Girl Reporter
Bytes Back!

SERIES

GET REAL #1:
Girl Reporter Blows Lid off Town!

GET REAL #2:
Girl Reporter Sinks School!

GET REAL #3:
Girl Reporter Stuck in Jam!

GET REAL #4:
Girl Reporter Snags Crush!

GET REAL #5:
Ghoul Reporter Digs Up Zombies!

GET REAL #6:
Girl Reporter Rocks Polls!

GET REAL #7:
Girl Reporter Gets the Skinny!

GET REAL #8:
Girl Reporter Bytes Back!

GET REAL #8

Girl Reporter Bytes Back!

Created by
LINDA ELLERBEE

HarperCollins*Publishers*

My deepest thanks to Katherine Drew, Anne-Marie
Cunniffe, Lori Seidner, Holly Camilleri, Whitney
Malone, Roz Noonan, Alix Reid, Julia Richardson,
and Susan Katz, without whom this series of books
would not exist. I also want to thank Christopher
Hart, whose book, *Drawing on the Funny Side of
the Brain*, retaught me how to cartoon. At age 11,
I was better at it than I am now. Honest.

Girl Reporter Bytes Back!
Copyright © 2001 by Lucky Duck Productions, Inc.
Produced by By George Productions, Inc.
Library of Congress Cataloging-in-Publication Data
Ellerbee, Linda.
    Girl reporter bytes back! / created by Linda Ellerbee.
        p.   cm. — (Get real ; #8)
    Summary: School newspaper reporter Casey Smith tries to uncover
who's behind the counterfeit Alienhead toys being auctioned on the
Real News website, and also discovers there are good and bad aspects
of Internet filtering.
    ISBN 0-06-440952-X (pbk.) — ISBN 0-06-029258-X (lib. bdg.)
    [1. Auctions—Fiction.   2. Internet—Safety measures—Fiction.
3. Journalism—Fiction.   4. Schools—Fiction.]   I. Title.
PZ7.E42845 Ghf   2001   00-057264
[Fic]—dc21   CIP
                                                                     AC
Typography by Carla Weise
1   2   3   4   5   6   7   8   9   10
❖
First Edition

For the kids,
who always get real

News Flash! Money Makes the World Go 'Round!

MY NAME IS Casey Smith, and I'm downloading for dollars.

Sitting at the computer in the *Real News* office, I was finally getting the appeal of those annoying TV game shows. You know, the ones where you watch people drool over the chance to win *mucho dinero*. One minute you're an average broke bloke (to use Brit-speak like my Brit-pal Melody), and then presto chango! Easy Street!

At the moment, I was online checking out the special *Real News* auction site. I wanted to see how high the price had gone for my contribution. Of course, any dollars it reeled in wouldn't be mine. But going to *Real News* was as good as landing in my pocket. The newspaper matters that much to me.

We were at the height of fund-raising month at Trumbull Middle School. That meant all of the school clubs were knocking their brains out trying to come up with sure-fire ways to rake in the dough.

"Club" is so not the word for *Real News*. We don't sit around thinking up cutesy themes for school dances or meet to discuss the finer points of Nintendo (as if there are any!) No—we provide an important service publishing the news each and every week, going where no kids have gone before. Or at least, where Trumbull students haven't gone in the last few years. Last year the school newspaper was declared defunct: canceled for lack of interest.

Until I showed up. I changed all that, resurrecting the newspaper.

Okay, so I didn't do it completely on my own. Megan O'Connor, our editor in chief, also had journalism fever. Only she and I don't always see eye to eye on what constitutes news. In my eyes, new shades of pink unleashed on the unsuspecting world do not a news story make. To balance out our yin-yang, we were joined by ring-a-ding Ringo as resident cartoonist, attitudinal Toni Velez as a crack photographer, and jock-of-all-trades, Gary Williams, sports writer. We had our bases covered.

Everyone (well, almost) loves *Real News*. We're a hit. Our problem was money. In fact, our already minuscule budget had been slashed—and first semester wasn't even over yet.

So there was a lot riding on this fund-raiser. We could use new computers, a printer, better paper. Even some pencils would be nice. Our idea was an online auction. Cool, huh? Especially since the real ones are so popular. Kids aren't allowed to bid on those, so we figured they'd go for ours big-time. We did get a lot of donations, with *Real News* receiving twenty-five percent of each sale. We had a hunch that no one would donate anything unless they got to keep most of the money. Each of us on staff also donated items, and a hundred percent of those sales would go straight to *Real News*.

The way the auction worked was this: We created a link from the school site where kids could post things they wanted to sell and other kids could bid on them. Because money was involved, everything was closely monitored. Our faculty advisor, Mr. Baxter, insisted on that. Any kid wanting to sell something had to fill out a form that was signed by a parent. After the bidding was finished, the kid who bought the item brought the money to Mr. Baxter, along with another permission slip from a parent. Mr. Baxter is big on permission slips. I guess that's what faculty advisors are for: getting grown-ups to sign things.

Once Mr. Baxter had the money, and took the *Real News* cut, the seller got an e-mail to come and pick up the moolah.

I was checking on the bids for my donation. I was sure it would be a winner. I had gotten Gram to autograph a copy of her prize-winning book, *After Watergate: The Loss of Innocence in American Politics.*

Gram was staying with me for a whole year while my parents were away. My parents are doctors with this cool organization called Doctors Without Borders. They travel all over the world and help wherever doctors are needed. Right now they're in Southeast Asia. They took my sixteen-year-old brother, Billy, with them. They said it would be a "cultural experience." I say it was so that Billy wouldn't experience flunking out of high school. He sure was heading that way.

The way I see it, I'm the one with the better deal. It's Journalism Central at my house—my dream life. Having Gram around makes things a lot more interesting here in Abbington, Massachusetts. The Berkshire Mountains are pretty and everything, but scenery only goes so far.

Now I wanted to bring a little of that dream-life to Trumbull Middle School. Between *Real News* and Gram's book for the auction, middle school kids could get a taste of what it was to be me, Casey Smith, reporter.

I scrolled through the auction listings. It was like an online garage sale. I spotted a used bicycle, clothes, toys, a few skateboards. Bo-ring! I figured Gram's book should really stand out among all the Alienheads trading cards and back issues of *Teen People*.

Funny. Gram had tried to talk me out of donating the book. She claimed middle school kids wouldn't be interested. I told her she was just being modest. Who wouldn't want an autographed copy of a book written by a famous journalist?

Well, it turned out—exactly no one.

I stared at the computer screen. I couldn't believe it. The bids were absolutely zilch. A total of zero customers for Gram's prize-winning book.

What were these fools buying? I checked the bids. The hottest-selling items were dorky Alienheads figurines. Sheesh.

Alienheads was this blockbuster sci-fi movie. It was all right, I guess. Fun, even. Okay, I admit it—I liked the stupid movie. I actually saw it twice. But I'm not into all the tie-in stuff: trading cards, backpacks, CD-ROM games, key rings, you name it. The biggest deals are the Alienheads figurines. They've become monster hits, collectibles even. That means they're now worth more money than you paid for them. Some of them, anyway. There are even books about how to collect them. You know the Beanie Babies and Pokémon phenoms? Then you've got an idea of the mania. Some of the figurines are really elaborate interactive doo-hickies; others are just models of characters in the movie. Kids eat them up, trying to collect them all or pick up rare pieces.

Obviously, Trumbull Middle Schoolers were more interested in two-headed bug-eyed plastic dolls than in Gram's hard-hitting, truth-telling book. What was wrong with these people?

I got up and paced twice around our big polka-dot table, aka Dalmatian Station. I kicked one of the table legs. Gram's book should have started a bidding war. Instead it was being totally dissed. Worse—how much money could *Real News* make if all that sold were little plastic critters?

I sat back down and double-checked the site. None of the Alienheads were going for more than five bucks a pop. The *Real News* take? A whopping buck twenty-five!

Let's see. That adds up to a box of pens.

I was afraid if I kept watching the auction site I'd start foaming at the mouth, so I surfed over to

Wheelies's Web World. I'd gotten into checking out Wheelies's site recently. It linked to the school homepage, like the *Real News* auction. It was devoted to "Truth, Freedom, and the Wheelies Way" and had lots of net tips. The "Gripes" column was what I read it for. Wheelies used it to sound off about whatever was bothering him or her that day. Wheelies had a definite way with words. As Gram would say, Wheelies had "a voice."

Wheelies also had a link to KidSpeak—an online chat for kids under sixteen. I've sometimes lurked there, but most of it goes by too fast for me and I can't keep up. Hate that. Besides, I'd rather have my conversations face-to-face. Still, Wheelies postings were often good for a laugh.

There were also links from Wheelies's Web World to game sites, a tech-help site and 'NSYNC and Backstreet Boys fan pages. Hm. I think I just got a clue that Wheelies was a girl.

I was reading Wheelies's latest, a riff on reruns (she's opposed), when I noticed the mail icon flashing. *Real News* had just received a message. Maybe it was a huge offer on Gram's book. I quickly clicked open the mail.

No such luck. It was the Monday afternoon update from the administrative office on the fund-raising activities of the previous week. They sent it out to all the clubs.

Boogers! *Real News* was dead last. Every other group had made more than us. How were we going to move up to the top of the list if only things like the cheapo Alienheads stuff attracted bids?

I needed to vent. Too bad I didn't have a column like "Gripes" to register my complaints. At least I had the perfect electronic ear—my friend Griffin.

Even though he moved miles and miles away last summer, Griffin and I still connected nearly daily via the internet. With Griff, e-mail is almost as good as an up-close and personal. I think that's because I know him so well. I can hear his voice in my head as I read his messages. I know exactly how to take anything he writes. Same thing on his end—the clear transmission works both ways.

I clicked open a new mail message and sounded off.

To: Thebeast
From: Wordpainter
Re: Interest in Alienheads proves low IQ !!!
    Has Alienheads stupidity invaded your school? Don't get me wrong—I liked the movie. (Remember the part where the little Alienheads totaled the big Alienheads

with Jell-O?) But all the commercial junk is ridiculous.

How dumb does a kid have to be to go bonkers collecting the tie-ins? Don't they realize all they're doing is paying for the privilege of advertising for a multi-million-dollar corporation? They should pay <u>us</u> to wear their T-shirts. I don't want to be a walking billboard. And why would anyone need a little toy whose eyes spin while it croaks "Humans are toast"? I mean, please. It was cute in the movie, but I don't want to hear it twenty times a day.

Tell me you aren't one of the brain-dead. If you are, I'll try to arrange an intelligence transplant for you.

"I picked up some new Head-Poppers," Toni Velez said as she entered the office with Ringo. "My collection is almost complete." She dropped her backpack onto the table and began rummaging through it.

"Awesome," Ringo replied. "Do you think Head-Poppers would eat Pop-Tarts for breakfast?" He plopped down onto the floor near me. "What do you think, Casey?"

Astonishing. The Alienheads obsession had

reached its tentacled claws into the *Real News* office. "I don't know and I don't care." I shook my head in disgust.

Megan O'Connor came in, dressed like a pink-and-white candy cane. "Casey, already writing up a story?" she asked.

I signed my rant to Griffin and hit Send. The e-mail message vanished into Cyberland. "No—" I began; then Gary's energized entrance cut me off.

"Check it out!" Gary declared. "The basketball team has totally scored with the raffle. Which happened to be my idea." His eyes sparkled with excitement against his dark skin. He was highly jazzed.

Gary's basketball team was raffling off tickets to some upcoming pro game. I'm told the game is an important one—if that sort of thing matters. The tickets were donated by the father of one of Gary's fellow jocks. The dad works for one of the teams. Our team was selling raffle tickets every day at lunch, making big bucks.

Gary's news burned me. Why couldn't Gary have gotten the tickets for us to sell through the auction?

"What about *Real News?*" I demanded. "Don't you want to know how we're doing? Or how we're *not* doing?"

"So how *are* we doing?" Megan asked from the

head of Dalmation Station. She totally clashed. Polka dots and stripes! I was surprised she didn't paint the table.

"Our numbers are in the basement," I told them. I turned back around to face the computer screen. The mail icon was flashing again. I clicked it open and saw my message to Griffin. My jaw dropped to my lap. How could that have happened?

I checked the address. Oh no! I had been distracted when I sent the mail. I didn't hit New Message. I hit Reply to All Recipients.

I just sent my anti-Alienheads rant as a reply to the administrative memo.

My message had just landed in the in-box of the administration—and every club at Trumbull.

New Study Proves It—You *Can* Die From Embarrassment!

MY SCALP PRICKLED under my hair as I stared at the screen. My face flamed as red as my Converse sneakers—and that's *red*. My perfect seashell ears felt hot. I could hear everyone talking around me, but they sounded like they were underwater.

Any minute now the entire school would know exactly how I felt about Alienheads.

This was not good.

Man! Why isn't there any way to retrieve that message? I thought. Can't I delete it or recall it somehow?

Nope. There was no Erase in Retrospect button on the keyboard.

Someone should invent one, I thought. That person would be a multizillionaire.

Well, that person wasn't me. There was nothing

I could do about it now, except wait for the consequences. I tuned back in to the conversation that had continued around me.

"I had to walk three dogs last night," Megan was explaining. "Then deliver newspapers this morning. I'm exhausted. But by the time the fundraiser is over, I think the yearbook will have made enough money to print in color this year."

"Selling chores has gone over big for you guys," Gary observed. "Decent."

"The cheerleaders are washing cars," Ringo said. He's an alternate on the cheerleading squad. A fact that I continually have to process. A cool, interesting, fun guy on the fluff squad? The information still does not compute. "We cheer while we do chores. It makes the time go faster."

"How much money has your team made?" Toni asked Gary.

Gary grinned, setting off dimple action. A lot of girls think Gary is cute. Sure he is, if you go for egomaniac jocks. Which I don't.

"We've already sold over two hundred raffle tickets," Gary announced proudly.

"At two bucks a ticket?" I said. "You made over four hundred dollars for a stupid *team*?"

"It's not stupid," Gary snapped. "Just because you're not into it, that doesn't mean it's dumb. Besides, we need equipment and uniforms."

"What about *Real News*?" I glared at all of them. "Am I the only one who cares about raising money for our newspaper? You people have your priorities all wrong."

"That's unfair, Casey," Megan scolded me. "We are perfectly capable of caring about more than one activity."

"Yeah," Gary added. "Just because your measly little brain can only process one thing at a time doesn't mean we're as limited as you."

I scrunched up my face at him. He scrunched back.

"It's not just about the money," Ringo said. "It's the totality of the event. The cheerleaders wash cars, and that makes people cheerful. So we're spreading the cheeriness of the squad through our actions."

"It is totally about the money, man," Toni scoffed. "Casey's right. We need to get on it, or *Real News* will blow this opportunity to make some bucks."

"Thank you, Toni," I said. "At least somebody here understands the importance of this fund-raiser."

"I wish the comic book collection I posted was doing better," she said.

"The only items doing well are Alienheads," I reported.

"That figures." Toni grinned. "They're awesome." She pulled several Alienheads from her backpack and stood them in a row on the table. She handled them as if they were precious gems.

"Are you donating those to the auction?" I asked eagerly.

"Are you nuts?" Toni said. "I just bought these. I've been looking for Head-Poppers for weeks."

I never would have pegged Toni for an Alienheads nut. She's always struck me as far too level-headed. Of course, some of the Alienheads kind of sounded like her. Maybe she related. The little ones have major attitude and the best comeback lines. And she's totally into special effects. Anything using a camera catches Toni's attention. Photography of all kinds is major with her.

But why that would translate into collecting action figures totally escapes me.

"Well, I think we should stop worrying about the auction and start worrying about next week's issue," Megan said. She pulled out her pink notebook and purple felt-tip pen. "All this talk about money has given me an idea."

She turned to me. "Casey, why don't you write about school funding? We'll cover the fund-raising activities, of course, but I think we could broaden the scope. Get into the issues of allocation on the local and statewide level."

I was surprised. Megan's idea was good. Usually she goes for much tamer stuff. Homecoming dances, school plays, that kind of thing. But her generosity made me suspicious. Megan may appear cream-puffy, but underneath that marshmallow exterior beats a—well, beats a candy-coated heart. But it shares artery space with a competitive news reporter.

"Why do you want me to write this up?" I asked.

She looked a little uncomfortable. "Well, it could turn into a big story. I just don't think I'll have time this week."

I narrowed my brown eyes and bored them right into her blue ones. "And why is that?"

She sighed. "I have so many extra chores because of the yearbook fund-raiser. My schedule already has me spinning."

Before I could slam her for her divided loyalties, Ringo called from his spot at the other computer. "Hey, Casey," Ringo asked. "Why is there a message from you in the *Real News* in-box?"

Oh no! The misdelivered message to Griffin. Of course. *Real News* was on that list of recipients.

"Just delete that!" I ordered Ringo.

"Why are you writing about Alienheads?" he asked, sounding puzzled.

16

"Alienheads?" Toni repeated. "Read it to us."

"No!" I jumped up. But before I could stop him, Ringo read the whole message. Out loud. Including the bit about an intelligence transplant.

Toni's eyes flashed with fury. I swear, sparks seemed to fly out of them, just like in *Alienheads*. Even her wild, long curls looked mad at me.

"Who put you in charge of the world?" Toni fumed.

"I-I-I—" I sputtered.

"You're the one who needs the brain transplant," she continued. She rose out of her chair and leaned across the table toward me. She grabbed the biggest Alienhead. I thought she was going to bean me with it.

I shouldn't have worried. She wouldn't risk damaging the precious creature. Me, on the other hand, she'd be happy to smash to pieces. I could tell.

"You think you're so smart," she yelled. She gestured at me with the Alienhead. "You always have to . . ." She stopped yelling and glanced at the critter. Her dark brows knit together.

She studied the Alienhead. I wasn't sure what was going on, but I was glad that she had stopped blasting me. She just kept squeezing the Alienhead's feet. Her expression went from puzzled to frantic.

"Is something wrong?" Megan asked.

Toni ignored the question. She picked up each of the Alienheads figurines, inspecting them closely. She squeezed their feet, tapped their heads, did everything except pull out a stethoscope to check if they were breathing.

"Toni, are your Alienheads sick or something?" Ringo asked.

"Worse." She held up the biggest figurine. "They're fake!"

Will the Real Alienheads Please Stand Up?

WE STARED AT the Alienheads.

"What do you mean, fake?" Gary asked.

"When I squeeze the feet the head is supposed to open up so that the little head inside can pop out." She squeezed the feet of the largest Alienhead. "But nothing happens. See?" She picked up each of the others. "Nothing at all."

"Maybe they're just broken," Megan suggested.

"All of them?" Toni demanded.

Toni picked up the big one again and peered at the bottom of its webbed feet. She let out a dismayed groan. "The logo is wrong. The real ones have a little Alienhead in the top part of the 'A.' These have the Alienhead in the bottom of the 'A.'"

"Wow." Gary picked one up. "They look so real. Exactly like the ones in the stores."

"Not exactly," Ringo commented. He held the smallest one on the palm of his hand. "If I remember the movie right, this little dude had six eyes. This guy's only got four."

Toni slumped down into a chair and rested her head in her hands. "I spent so much money on these," she wailed. "I thought they were really rare! I even borrowed on my allowance."

"We'll get your money back," Megan assured her. "The person who sold them probably didn't realize."

"Oh, they knew," Toni grumbled. "They were advertised as Head-Poppers. You see any popping heads here? Do you?"

We all shook our heads.

"I'm letting this scam artist know whose head is going to pop." She stalked over to Ringo's computer. He got up, and Toni sat down. Her eyes narrowed as she gazed at the screen. "And after that, I'll deal with you," she snarled in my direction.

Great. Ringo must have left my e-mail on the screen. Just what I didn't need. I had hoped that Toni would forget about my anti-Alienheads rant in all the excitement of getting ripped off.

She clicked on the mouse, then typed what seemed to be an extremely brief message. She got up and paced. She looked ready to smack some-thing. I really didn't want it to be me.

"We'll straighten this out," Megan assured Toni. She came over to my computer. I scurried out of the chair. I wasn't going to interfere with solving Toni's problem. I was in enough hot water with her as it was.

Megan hit a bunch of keys. "Okay, I've pulled up the list of items," she said. "If you get no response to your e-mail, we'll make a call. What was the seller's name?"

Everything being sold was carefully logged in by item and listed both the person's screen name and real name, another bit of paperwork Mr. Baxter had insisted on. Now I could see why.

Toni stared at her hands. She twirled her bangle bracelets around and around her wrist. "I-I didn't buy them through the *Real News* auc-tion," she confessed.

Traitor! I thought. What was she doing buying from a different site, one that didn't give *Real News* a cut?

"Where did you get them?" Megan asked.

"Someone posted them for sale on the regular school online bulletin board."

There was an online bulletin board linked to the school homepage. Kids posted all kinds of things: everything from birthday greetings, to requests for volunteers, to homework help. I usually only skimmed it. I figured as a reporter I should keep on top of what kids might post, but there was never anything too interesting there.

"Then just go over to the kid's house and confront him," Gary suggested.

Toni looked embarrassed. I rarely saw this side of her. She looked as if she was shrinking in her chair, like the Alienhead that kept getting smaller every time she did something wrong.

"I don't know who sold it," Toni said. "I don't even know if it was a boy. I just know the name, GoForIt, and a post office box."

"You didn't hand over the money in person?" Megan asked.

Toni shook her head. "I sent the cash to a post office box, and the Alienheads arrived a few days later."

I raised an eyebrow. Toni was such a savvy chick. She wasn't the type I'd peg as a target for a scam. But everything about this setup screamed con. "Didn't any of this raise a red flag?" I asked. "I mean, cash to a post office box. It's a dead giveaway."

Toni stood and placed her hands on her hips. "Oh, of course! Dumb Toni gets cheated. That's because anyone into Alienheads is too stupid to know better, right? That's what you think, right?

Well, you know what? I don't care what you think."

She stormed out of the room. Everyone stared after her.

I felt two opposing feelings at the same time. My stomach and chest were tight from having Toni so mad at me and being yelled at in front of everybody. My ears, nose and fingers tingled the way they always do when I'm onto a news story.

The reporter feelings won out. "This is great!" I exclaimed.

"Great?" Ringo repeated, dumbfounded. "You think it's great that Toni got ripped off?"

"No, no, not *that*," I assured him. "It's a great story. Online scams—right here at Trumbull. There's been stuff all over the news about this kind of thing. Now we can take on the issue ourselves."

"We don't know that it was a scam," Megan protested. "Everyone is innocent until—"

"Blah, blah, blah," I finished for her. I'd heard it before.

"Well, it's true!" Megan said, all huffy. "We don't know if the seller realized the Alienheads weren't what Toni had expected. Besides, a single incident does not add up to a criminal ring."

"I'm with Casey on this," Gary said.

23

"I'm stunned," I said. I gave him a mock shocked expression. "We agree."

He gave me a light punch on the arm. "For once." He tipped back in his chair. "Toni is never getting a dime back. And taking how mad she is as a clue, I'd say she paid plenty for these things. I've seen how pricey the Alienheads stuff can get. I checked it out when I was deciding what to donate to the *Real News* auction."

"You're into Alienheads, too?" I asked. Was I the only nonclueless one here? Actually, Alienheads might be the only area where Megan and I had common ground. I don't think she even saw the movie. The creatures weren't cute or cuddly, so she wouldn't go for them. If they were pink, furry and covered in glitter, maybe. But not slimy, scaly, bug-eyed aliens that spit at you. Not her style.

"Not much," Gary replied. "That's why I donated my cards to the auction."

That got me back to worrying about how badly *Real News* was doing in the fund-raising department. "You know, if we don't get some money, it's not going to matter how great our stories are. Not if we can't afford to buy paper to print them on."

"It's not going to come to that," Megan said.

"Okay," I declared. "Let's settle this. What has everyone donated?"

"The Alienheads stuff I donated sold instantly," Gary reminded me.

"Let me check on the other items," Megan said. She clicked on to the site. "Casey, your grandmother's book still doesn't have a bid."

Rub it in, why don't you? I thought. "I know. But I'm sure they'll start bidding soon. They probably just need to get their parents to give them permission to bid so high." If only. I crossed my fingers for luck.

"Let's see," Megan murmured. "There's a bid on the comic book collection Toni donated, but it's not for much. I think she was figuring it would bring in more than that."

"We need more than a few measly dollars," I complained. "Wait a sec. What about your donation?" I asked Megan.

Her Pinkness blushed pink. "I haven't thought of anything yet," she confessed.

"Well, get thinking!" I ordered. "What are you waiting for? Or is raising money for the yearbook all that's on your mind?"

"Casey, I'll think of something, okay? Just quit hounding me."

Amazing. She actually lost her temper. This was a rare phenomenon. She must be stressing.

I decided to back off Megan. I figured guilt would work its way into her system and she'd come up with some extra-special donation that would rake in the big bucks. Instead I honed in on Ringo.

He must have known he was next. He sat with

Well, you said you wanted
to make Big Money!

his back to me, doodling. "Wanna see my newest Simon?"

"That's cute, Ringo," I said. "But you're not backing out. What's going on with your donation?"

Ringo had promised a self-published cookbook, complete with his own cartoon illustrations. The plus side was that he could print up as many as he needed. He didn't like the whole competition aspect of bidding. Weird, since he competes in cheerleading competitions and roots at sporting events.

"I only have a few recipes to go," Ringo promised.

"What's the holdup?" I asked.

"Well, I decided it would sell better if it wasn't strictly vegetarian," he explained. "But my parents are. Strictly veggie. So I need to include some meat recipes."

"Well, let's take care of that right now," I said. I gestured at the computer. "There are plenty of cooking sites. Do a keyword search and get some recipes to use as inspiration."

I had a feeling if I didn't push him, it would get postponed while he washed more cars into cheerfulness—benefiting who? The Cheerios. I decided not to let him out of my sight until the cookbook was complete.

I dragged my chair over beside him. "Go on," I said, "get some chicken recipes."

"I should be more specific than chicken," he said. "Otherwise, I might come up with famous cowards or farming sites."

"Good idea," I said.

"My mom uses chicken breasts because they cook fast," Megan suggested. "Quick recipes are popular."

Popular. Exactly what we were looking for. "Try that," I said.

He went into the keyword search option and typed in "chicken breasts."

"Huh?" He stared at the screen. "'Access Denied?'"

"Talk about secret recipes," I commented. "What's up with this?"

Instead of bringing up loads of search results, the computer said that our search included words from "blocked sites."

Blocked sites. That could only mean one thing. The school had installed software that determined where a user could and couldn't go on the net.

Yowza! Internet censorship. Right here on the computer in the *Real News* office.

Today was a reporter's dream day. I didn't have to go out in search of stories this week. This week they were marching right into the office and grabbing me!

Just Say Know!

"THIS IS THE story I want to cover," I told Megan. "Censorship on the Net."

"What about the online scam story you just pitched?" Megan demanded.

"I'll write that story, too," I said. "They kind of go together—Internet issues in the brave new online world, or something like that."

Megan pursed her gloss-dabbed lips. "That's a good point. We're becoming more wired every day."

"Exactly," I said. "This is an issue that affects everyone, not just the tech-heads."

"It's a good idea. Go for it. But . . ." Megan waggled her purple pen at me. "I'll expect a balanced story. This isn't just a First Amendment rant. You have to research all sides of the issues. And keep in mind that there may not be a scam at all. Simply an honest mistake."

Typical Megan. She always has to remind me who's in charge. Right now I didn't care. I had the stories I wanted, each with the kind of edge I like. Issues that really affected kids like me—and everyone else. Far-reaching. Hard-hitting. Non-fluffy and antiboring. I could cut her some slack. This time.

I gave her a little salute. "Yes, sir!" I said.

Now if someone would just bid big bucks on Gram's book, today would be total aces.

"Come on, my cheery chef," I told Ringo. "Let's try the school library for your chicken recipes." I knew they had an additional database. Once we were there, Ringo could finish up the cookbook and I could start researching the whole Internet censorship thing.

"Hi, Ms. Wexler," I said to the red-haired librarian. We headed for the row of computers. We were in luck. There wasn't a waiting list to get online.

"Maybe I should try doing a search for steak instead," Ringo whispered. I think he felt a little nervous about going after sites that we'd already been denied access to. What I couldn't understand was why they wouldn't want us to download recipes for chicken breasts? Was the Colonel worried that some middle schoolers would make a recipe to rival KFC and hurt his sales? Was there a conspiracy to turn us all into vegetarians? I couldn't figure it out.

It happened again. "'Access denied. Your search included words from a list of blocked terms,'" I read from the screen.

Okay, this was serious. What happened on the *Real News* office computer wasn't a fluke. It was a system-wide access denial. There was no on-ramp to this information superhighway.

We headed for Ms. Wexler. She was checking things off on an order form. I waited until she glanced up. "So what's up with all this access denied stuff?" I asked her.

She put down the catalogue. "What were you trying to do?" she asked. "You know you can't log on to games from the school library."

"We were looking for recipes," Ringo explained. "Only the computers won't give them up. They're stingier than my aunt Sarah and her recipe for vegetarian turkey." He tugged a strand of his shaggy brown hair. "You know, my dad thinks the secret ingredient is actual turkey."

Ms. Wexler gazed at Ringo for a moment, then looked at me. I noticed she had brown freckles across her nose just like mine. "What was the search word?" she asked me. I guessed she decided that between me and Ringo, I was the safer bet. "Perhaps you've misspelled something."

"How hard is it to spell chicken breasts?" I asked.

Ms. Wexler took a second, then chuckled. "I think I understand."

"What?" What was I missing here? Why were chicken nuggets suddenly as classified as instructions for nuclear bombs?

"The blocking software is reacting to the word 'breasts,'" she explained.

I instinctively covered my chest. My eyes flicked over to Ringo. Was he suddenly self-conscious, too?

Ringo looked puzzled. "So I wouldn't be able to research breast cancer either?"

Whoa. Good question. I should have asked it.

One of the things I like best about Ringo is that underneath all that trippy lingo and space-case persona lurks a truly synapse-snapping brain.

"Yeah," I said, jumping onto the issues band-wagon. "How can the library justify blocking *any* words? That's a form of censorship. It's like banning books!"

"It's an imperfect system," Ms. Wexler agreed. "But there do need to be safeties in place."

"To protect us from rampaging chicken breasts?" I asked.

"Maybe it's to protect the chickens," Ringo

suggested. "I mean, it's not so good for them if we publish lots of delicious recipes. We could wipe out the entire chicken population."

I could tell Ms. Wexler was trying to decide if we were being serious. What she didn't realize was that Ringo was dead serious. His mind just goes off on these tangents.

I got back on track. "What is this list?"

"The library has installed a software program that has a blocked sites list as well as a keyword filter. That means," she continued, noticing my blank expression, "that any sites pulled up as a result of a search that includes words or sites that are on those lists will be blocked. They won't appear—or the search itself will be canceled."

"So what about our search?" I demanded. "Just because it uses the word, uh, 'breast,' it got canceled?" I avoided Ringo's eyes. For some reason saying the word in front of a boy made me feel funny. Not funny ha-ha either.

"The word 'breast' appears on the list because it is used in many adults-only sites," Ms. Wexler explained. "The problem is that the computer doesn't distinguish between the inappropriate and appropriate sites. Hence, your chicken breast and breast cancer problem. However, there are plenty of books that include information on both subjects."

"Who made the decision to install the software?" I asked.

"The administration."

"The PTA didn't vote on it? Or the students?"

Ms. Wexler shrugged. "I don't make the rules."

This steamed me. Who are they to decide—filter—what we can and can't access!

And how were we going to finish Ringo's cookbook? Paging through cookbooks could take forever. A keyword search would be a snap.

Time to hit the home computers. There was no way that Gram or my parents would install blocking software. I knew exactly where they stood on First Amendment issues like this. Freedom of speech. The right to know. The right to information. That's what Gram's whole life has been based on.

"Come on, Ringo," I commanded. "Let's go to my house, where people understand the right of free speech."

"Good luck with your recipe research," Ms. Wexler said.

I had to hand it to her. She seemed pretty reasonable about the whole thing. She was apologetic about the hassle and didn't go all grown-up on me when I voiced my opinion. I decided to come back later and interview her for my story.

◆◆◆

"Hi, Gram," I called as we charged into my house.

"Hi, Casey," I heard from the study. Gram was using her time here to write her memoirs. That's how famous she is. So why wasn't anyone bidding on her Watergate book? The autograph alone had to be worth something.

"I've got Ringo with me," I added as we passed the study on the way to the stairs.

"Hi, Ringo," came through the door.

"Hi, door," Ringo replied. "And Casey's gram."

Ringo and I went up to my room. "Why are you so bugged about getting a cookbook collection together?" Ringo asked. "It's not like you have a dinner emergency or anything."

"Don't you get it?" I sat down at the computer and logged on. "The *Real News* auction is a bust. The cookbook is a good idea. Parents go for this sort of thing. And once you write it, we can sell as many as we want. We need to get it online tomorrow."

I typed in the keyword and clicked on Search.

"Look at all those hits!" Ringo exclaimed. "Who knew there were so many recipes for chicken breasts."

Ringo was right. There were a gazillion hits for the search. "Ha. No access denied here," I said.

There were so many! How would we choose a site or page to check out?

Ringo was thinking the same thing. He squinted at the screen. "Hey, here's one called 'Tasty.' That sounds promising. We want tasty recipes."

We clicked on to the link.

Boingo!

That was the sound my eyes made when they popped out of my head. I think I heard Ringo squeak next to me. Unless it was me. I know I made some kind of gross half swallow, half yelp sound in the back of my throat.

Right there on my very own computer. Right in front of my eyes. Right in front of Ringo.

An entire screen full of naked, well, *you-know-whats!*

And I don't mean chickens.

Nobody Here but Us Chickens!

Wow! You never know what you'll find on the World Wide Web!

MY FACE TURNED more shades of red than I knew existed. I snuck a peek at Ringo. His mouth had dropped open so far I could practically see his tonsils. He was even redder than I was. Except his ears, which had gone white.

I had to get us out of there! I reached for the mouse to click on to something—*anything* else! Only Ringo had exactly the same idea. Our hands hit, we clicked and double-clicked, and wham. More pix of naked boobs appeared. Like magic. Seriously twisted magic.

The door swung open behind us. "Casey, will Ringo be staying for dinner?" Gram asked.

Eeeeeekkk!

Ringo leaped toward the computer. I think he was trying to use his body as a shield. I leaped for the mouse. Somehow my chair knocked into Ringo's, and both of us tipped over. We landed in a heap on the floor.

Gram stared at us quizzically. "Is everything all right in here?"

I stretched out my fingers, trying to reach for the mouse as I scrambled back up. I reached . . . I reached . . .

Gram stepped over us and peered at the screen.

Busted. In both senses of the word.

"Ringo," she said very calmly. Much more calmly than I was feeling. "I think it would probably be a good idea if you went home now."

"Thank you. I mean, yes. I mean, sure thing. I mean, uh-huh." Ringo crawled a few feet across the floor, stumbled to his feet and raced out of the room. I heard the front door slam. If quick exits were an Olympic sport, Ringo would have just qualified for the team.

Man oh man. Now what was going to happen? What did Gram think? Did she imagine that Ringo and I were in here looking at that stuff on purpose?

"Gram, it was a total mistake!" I blurted. "We were trying to find recipes, and all these pictures showed up instead."

"First, let's take care of this." Gram reached over and logged off the net. She perched on the edge of my bed. "Now what exactly were you trying to find?"

I explained all about the chicken recipes and the blocking software at school.

"I never felt it was necessary to install any such software because I have always felt you displayed good judgment. I hope my trust in you wasn't misplaced."

"It's not," I assured her. "I swear."

She smiled. "I believe you. But you have to understand, there's a reason that this kind of software exists. I don't believe in it myself, but I understand the concerns that lead parents to install it. The Internet is full of people, just like the real world. And just as there are in the real world, there are good people and bad people. There are also appropriate places for kids to hang out, and places that they shouldn't. Just because it's only virtual, that doesn't mean it's okay for kids."

"But I didn't go there," I said. "They came to me."

I shuddered. It gave me the creeps that I could innocently ask the computer for a chicken recipe and all these naked pictures appeared instead.

"That's another reason for the software," Gram replied. "It wouldn't have allowed that to happen."

That would have been good. Only then I remembered Ringo's comment at the library. The filters would have blocked the nudie stuff, but it would have blocked other things as well. "But I wouldn't get any hits on breast cancer either," I said.

"True," Gram said. "It is a complicated decision."

It sure was.

"I know you use the Internet a lot, and it is a valuable tool," Gram said. "But like any tool, if it's not used properly it can be dangerous. So let's talk a little about the rules, okay?"

She patted the bed beside her.

Once again I appreciated how cool Gram was.

Another adult might have gone ballistic before finding out the backstory.

I sprawled out next to her. I felt sort of comforted that we were going over this internet stuff. It suddenly seemed like the Wild West out there, with all roads leading right into my room.

"Okay, the most important thing is behavior in chat rooms," she said. "Do you go to chat rooms?"

"Sometimes," I answered. "The one from Wheelies's Web World."

She nodded. "The one for kids." I'd shown her some of the stuff on Wheelies's web page, so she knew what it was about. "Good. That's the first rule. It's important to stick to chat rooms specifically aimed at the right age group. But even there, you have to remember that the person behind the screen name may not resemble your image. Someone calling himself 'Tough Dude' could be the shyest kid in your class. On the other hand, there can be adults online pretending to be kids."

I had never thought of that.

"You know the rules about being careful when you talk to strangers?" she asked. "Stay aware, trust your instincts if you feel uncomfortable, all that?"

"Uh-huh," I replied.

"Well, it's easy to forget online that those chatters are all strangers."

This was starting to creep me out big-time. I think she sensed that. "This may make you uncomfortable, but it's important that we talk about it," she said, smoothing my hair. "So the biggest rule of all—never, ever meet anyone in person that you meet online."

"Ever?" I asked. There were some kids who sounded really interesting online. Like Wheelies.

Gram smiled. "Okay. 'Never' is a big word. How about this. Never meet anyone without my permission. And if you do, it will be in a public place with an adult present."

"Like you?" I asked.

"Exactly like me. In fact, make it me."

"Deal." The way I was feeling right now, though, I didn't think I'd go online ever again.

"You know the rest of the drill—don't give out personal information unless you know exactly where you're sending it and to whom."

"Like the *Real News* auction site," I said. "Where I know who is using it and why."

"Right. As to appropriate web pages—well, I think I'll trust you on that one. You've already learned that things aren't always what they seem to be in cyberspace."

"You got that right." I sighed. "I don't think Ringo is ever going to be the same."

"I think he'll survive. So will you." She patted

my knee as she stood up. "Since you didn't find any recipes online, how about frozen pizza for dinner?" she said.

"Excellent."

After she left the room, I tiptoed over to the computer. I felt as if I had to be really careful about which buttons I clicked on. Otherwise who knew what would jump out and grab me?

This got me thinking about Toni and her fake Alienheads. It would be so easy to scam online— it's so anonymous. Gram should have given Toni the Internet lecture. Maybe then she wouldn't have gotten ripped off.

Which reminded me. I wondered if we were doing any better on the *Real News* auction. I logged onto the school homepage. Can you believe I was visiting the school site after hours after spending all day in the school? I must be crazy.

From the Trumbull homepage I clicked on to the *Real News* link. Hey—we had mail. A ton of it. I knew the auction would be a success once it got rolling.

Well, roll me over and stick a "Kick Me" sign on my butt. It was all hate mail. For me.

Word about my Alienheads rant had spread from the clubs to the entire school. Everyone replied right away to the message—which I had written from the *Real News* address.

Man. I had to sign my real name. I couldn't hide behind my screen name or anything. As if the *Real News* return address wasn't a dead giveaway.

This could turn into a loooooooooooong week.

Time Warp Exists—One School Day Equals an Eternity!

THE NEXT MORNING I popped into the *Real News* office. Maybe someone had bid on Gram's book between the time I checked on it at home and the time I got to school.

It could happen.

But it didn't.

I slumped in the chair in front of the computer, glaring at the little zero next to Gram's listing. How would Gram feel if I had to tell her that her book was a bust? *I* was totally bummed. I could only imagine how *she* would feel.

I had an idea. I got up and peeked out the doorway into the hallway. No one was on their way into the office. Sometimes Megan or Ringo drop by before classes. But the hallway was empty.

I dashed back to the computer and entered a bid on Gram's book. Just to stoke the fire. I posted a bid for $3.00—not too high, not too low. The way the bidding worked was that a kid would e-mail a bid to *Real News* and then we'd enter the amount. So no one saw the name of the bidder on the auction site—just the amount of the bid.

I grinned at the screen. Three dollars looked so much better than zero.

I was happy to see that I hadn't received any new hate mail. Last night I had picked up and deleted twenty-three messages slamming me for what I wrote to Griffin about Alienheads.

I smacked my forehead. Griffin! He never got the message—since I sent it through the entire school instead. Hm. Maybe I'd wait to write to him until I get home. I didn't want to risk a repeat of yesterday's e-mail disaster.

While I was online I came up with a good idea for researching the Internet censorship story. I posted a question to the student online bulletin board:

Did you know that your school computer system uses blocking and filtering software? That means there is software installed that decides what you can and can't see.

**How do you feel about Internet block-
ing and filtering programs?**

**Do you have it on your computer at
home?**

**Has it had an impact on you? Do you
think it's good or bad?**

I added that they should reply to the *Real News*
address and to tell me if they wanted to be quoted
or if I should use their comments anonymously.

The first bell rang. I logged off and grabbed
my backpack. I had to hit my locker before homeroom.

I got to my locker, and what did I find? A big
Alienheads sticker. Some clever kid had added
a sign saying "Casey, YOU'RE the REAL Alienhead!!!!"

Real mature.

While I scraped the stupid thing off with my
fingernails, Toni passed by. I knew the dis wasn't
hers. If Toni had something to say, she'd say it
straight to my face.

"Hey, Toni," I greeted her.

She snapped her gum and glared at me.

"Have you heard from GoForIt yet? Are you
getting your money back?" I asked. I hoped that
the problem had been solved. I figured that might
make her stop being mad at me.

Toni's eyes flashed. "No," she said. "And I know what you're thinking. Anyone stupid enough to be into Alienheads is stupid enough to get ripped off." She turned and stomped away.

"That's not true," I called after her as she vanished into the crowd of kids.

I trudged to homeroom. Will Toni ever like me again? I wondered.

I didn't have too long to worry about it. The minute my butt hit the chair, a hall monitor came in with a note summoning me to the principal's office.

Oh joy. Could this day get any better?

As I walked with the monitor to Principal Nachman's office I scrolled though my brain's hard drive, trying to figure out what caused this command appearance. I pulled up a mental file: the misdirected e-mail.

Principal Nachman was waiting for me at her desk. "Well, Casey, you seem to be something of a regular here. Perhaps we should designate a special chair just for you." Principal Nachman smiled, but I wasn't so sure it was a joke.

"I have a feeling you know why you're here," she continued.

"Not exactly," I said. I knew enough to reveal as little information as possible. Why bring up the e-mail if I was here for some completely different reason?

Principal Nachman sighed. She probably had hoped I'd make this meeting easier for her. Fat chance. "Casey, I'm sure you understand the importance of proper use of school computers. The system is a privilege for students, and if you abuse that privilege it can and will be revoked. It isn't your personal message center."

"It was an accident," I protested. "Do you really think I wanted the entire school to read that e-mail?"

"Perhaps you should keep in mind that the system at school is for school-related purposes," Principal Nachman continued. "That e-mail message should have been sent on your own time, from your personal computer."

"I know," I grumbled. "Believe me, I'm paying for this big-time."

I couldn't believe it! I actually saw a teeny little smile playing across Principal Nachman's lips. She was enjoying this!

"I can imagine," she said. "However, I felt I needed to remind you about appropriate and inappropriate use of the school computers."

"Well, cheating kids over the Internet is an inappropriate use of school computers, too," I blurted. "But are you doing anything about that?

No, you're lecturing *me*. All I did was make a dumb mistake, which the entire student body is going to make me regret."

Principal Nachman looked stunned. Obviously my little outburst caught her off guard. It caught me off guard, too. I mean, for all I knew Megan was right, and what had happened to Toni was an honest mistake.

"What are you talking about?" she asked me. "Who has been cheated? How?"

Great. The last thing Toni would want is to be hauled down and questioned by the principal. I was sure she wouldn't want it to get around school that she'd been ripped off either. If word got out about the incident because of me, I could kiss off any hope of her being my friend again.

"Casey? I'm waiting. What exactly did you mean? Has someone been cheated because of the auction?"

"*What?* No!" I shouted. I was afraid that Principal Nachman would cancel the *Real News* auction. Then where would we be?

She raised an eyebrow. Grown-ups don't like it when kids yell at them. Principals are no exception.

"Sorry. It's just that I didn't want you think *Real News* had anything to do with this. All I know is that someone bought some rare Alienheads from the regular school bulletin board. Only they weren't rare. They weren't even real Alienheads. They were knockoffs."

"That is serious." Principal Nachman waggled a pen between her fingers, then tapped it on her desk. "I'll check into it. Thank you."

"Can I go?" The choice between hanging in the principal's office and missing the first part of math was a no-brainer. I'd take pop quizzes from the Terminator over even the simplest conversation with Principal Nachman any day.

Principal Nachman nodded. "Good luck," she called as I reached for the doorknob. I glanced back. That little smile was there again.

If Principal Nachman enjoyed the idea that I was getting heat because of that stupid e-mail, she would have loved my morning. Kids passed Alienheads notes to me in class. They whispered "brain transplant" as I passed in the hall.

Was I the only kid at Trumbull who wasn't obsessed by Alienheads? Maybe that movie wasn't fiction. Maybe it was a documentary. Alienheads had taken over the human population, just like in the movie, and I was the only non-Alien left.

At lunch I scoped out the cafeteria. Rats. Ringo and his fellow Cheerios were doing some lunchtime car-washing, so I wouldn't have him to sit with. I didn't see Melody anywhere—I think she was painting sets for the drama club. I'd even have been willing to sit with Megan, but she was a no-show, too. Probably running some kind of errand, bringing in the bucks for the yearbook.

This was going to be a lonely lunch. Change that from lonely to annoyingly obnoxious. Someone hit me in the head with a wad of paper. I unsquished it and read the message "Alienheads Rule, You're a Fool!"

I glanced at my tray. Maybe I could get my lunch to go. I could hang out in the *Real News* office where it was safe. Then I heard something that caught my attention.

"These Alienheads are totally bogus! I got cheated."

I scanned the nearby table for the speaker. I spotted a sixth-grade boy with a buzz cut showing an Alienheads figurine to his friends. I hurried over.

"Hi, I'm Casey," I said. "Did you say you bought a fake Alienhead?"

"Don't talk to her, Ben," another boy said. "She's the one who said anyone who likes Alienheads is stupid."

"Get over it," I snapped. "I'm trying to help your bud here."

I set my tray down on the table and slid into

the seat opposite Ben. "I know someone else who bought a fake Alienhead," I told him. "I want to track down the creep. The first thing I have to figure out, though, is if your creep the same as her creep."

"Do you really think you can find GoForIt?" Ben asked. "Because I shelled out a lot of money for this Wacky Walker and it doesn't walk."

Jackpot! "You bought this from GoForIt?" I asked. "That was the same name my friend told me. Did you get it from the school bulletin board?"

Ben nodded.

"Did you send cash to a post office box?"

He nodded again.

"Let me see that Alienhead."

Ben handed me the figurine. It was about six inches tall, purple and green, with five legs. I remembered it from the movie—it couldn't walk in a straight line, so it was always bumping into things. I figured the toy was supposed to do the same thing.

It was a lot lighter than I thought it would be—a clear sign that there were no mechanisms inside to make it walk. I checked the logo. It didn't even have an Alienhead in the letter "A." Definitely fake.

"GoForIt got you, too," I declared.

"Tell me something I don't know," Ben grumbled. "I paid twenty-five dollars for that hunk of junk."

"Did you say you bought something from GoForIt?" a familiar voice said behind me.

I glanced up and sort of melted. Tyler McKenzie stood behind my chair, holding his lunch tray. He looked all . . . Tyler-y.

"I got ripped off, too," Tyler said.

Oh no. The warm squishy feeling in my stomach turned into tight knots. Tyler bought Alienheads. That meant he must be a fan. Had he heard about my anti-Alienheads e-mail? Did he hate me now, like everyone else on the planet?

"Hi, Tyler," I ventured. I waited to see if he'd slam me for my rant.

"Hi, Casey." He smiled at me, and there went that melty feeling again. I felt inside kind of the way my Halloween candy looked the time I left it on my radiator overnight.

"Mind if I sit?" He nodded toward the table.

Mind? "Sure, if you want to," I said. This was going well. I sensed no hostility. Which meant either he hadn't heard about the e-mail yet or he didn't care about it. I hoped, hoped, hoped the answer was choice B.

Tyler sat down next to me. "This is the fake one?" he asked Ben. Tyler examined the Alienhead.

Ben nodded.

"That's tough." Tyler put the critter back down and shook his head in sympathy.

"What did you buy?" I asked Tyler.

"I picked up a Head-Popper," Tyler said. "Only no popping."

"Why do you care?" the other boy at the table demanded. "You think anyone who is into this stuff is a dope."

I wanted to shrivel up into a little ball. I felt lower than the slimy gunk I pick out of the mystery stew. I tried to will him to shut up. Stop talking *now*, I ordered him with all of my brain power. I wanted to avoid any discussion of my opinion of Alienheads in front of Tyler.

"Oh man, I gotta run," Ben said. "I promised Tommy I'd go over the notes he missed last week. I was supposed to meet him at his locker ten minutes ago."

"I'll go with you," his friend said. "I don't want to sit with an enemy of Alienheads."

The magic mind meld wasn't working. Sheesh. This guy acted as if Alienheads were real and he was their special lieutenant. I wasn't sorry to see him leave with Ben.

Now that Tyler and I were alone at the table, I felt a little nervous. What if Tyler was just being nice to me because those two boys were sitting here? He was a polite guy.

I had to find out. I cut to the chase. "So you're into Alienheads?" I asked.

He shrugged. "I liked the movie," he replied.

I studied him for a minute. He seemed amused. He stared down at his food, but I could see he was trying not to smile.

"You heard, right?" I asked.

"About your totally nondiplomatic e-mail? Yeah." He grinned. "I figured the rumors were exaggerated."

That meant he hadn't read it, I realized. Because my message was exactly as bad as everyone was saying. Phew. Then I remembered he wasn't in any clubs. He wouldn't have had access to the original. Double phew.

"Besides," he went on, "it wasn't a big stretch to figure you wouldn't be into the Alienheads stuff. It's not your style." He took a bite of his roll, then a swig of soda.

He knew my style? Was that good or was that bad? I suppose that depended on what he thought my style was. Too bad I couldn't think of any way to ask him without coming across as a moony dork. So instead I attempted to swallow some stew.

"Anyway, I'm just bummed that the Alienhead I bought is fake," he said. "Now I can't give it to my cousin for his birthday. *He's* the Alienheads freak. That was the only reason I bought it. I'm not into collecting all that stuff."

"So did GoForIt get you to go for it, too?" I asked.

Tyler nodded. "I sent money to a post office box. It struck me as weird at the time, but I was kind of pressed for present ideas. I was in a hurry. What do you mean 'too'? Was someone else ripped off?"

"Uh, well." Now what had I done?

I'd seen enough of Toni's reaction to know that she wasn't going to appreciate anyone else knowing. But I didn't know how to get out of this. "Acually, Toni picked up some fake ones as well."

Suddenly, my news nose started tingling so much I practically needed a Kleenex. Toni wasn't going to like Tyler knowing, but this was a real story. I now had evidence that there was a scam artist operating on the Trumbull student bulletin board. That would be one major front-page story. It might even make it into the real newspaper— onto the wire services, across the national news syndicates!

I was getting ahead of myself. The first thing I had to do was track down GoForIt. Reveal the person behind the screen name.

"I'm going to find out who did this," I promised Tyler. "I'm going to blow this case wide open and print it all in *Real News.*"

"I'm there!" Tyler said. "Count me in."

"Truly?" I asked. "You'll help investigate?"

"Definitivo."

Tyler and I picked up our soda cans and clicked, making a toast. "To going for GoForIt," I declared.

Today was finally looking up!

CHAPTER 7

Real News Hits *Real News!*

It was tough making it through the rest of my classes. I wanted to get right to work on this story. It was a big one. I was practically percolating when I dashed into the *Real News* office.

Good! Megan and Toni were both already there. "Guess what!" I declared. "This Alienheads thing has turned into a serious story after all."

I plopped down beside Megan. "I did exactly what you said. I didn't just assume that GoForIt was guilty. But I tracked down two other kids who were scammed. And there are probably more out there." I beamed at Toni. "Isn't that great?"

Whoa. Serious miscalculation.

Toni's eyes narrowed. She crossed her arms over her chest and stuck out her lower lip. "Why would I think it's great that GoForIt ripped off

59

other kids? What is wrong with you?"

"I-I-I—" I sputtered.

"Oh, I get it. More proof of how stupid Alienheads fans are, right?"

"That is totally unfair," I protested. I looked over at Megan. Why wasn't she defending me? Her head was bowed, and she was peering at her notebook as if it held the secrets of the universe. I could see she wanted to stay out of it. No one ever wants to get in Toni's way when she's on a roll.

Including me. Still, I stood by my comments. "Look, if people want to waste their time and their money on dopey tie-ins, that's their business. I'm entitled to my opinion. No one was supposed to read that mail but my friend Griffin. So in a way, the entire school was eavesdropping. What I say in the privacy of my e-mail—"

"Can it," Toni snapped. "I have no interest in hearing you defend yourself. Because there is no defense. You are a totally insensitive dodo-head."

Before I could respond, Ringo walked in. The weirdest thing happened to me. I clammed up. As soon as I saw him, those dumb naked pictures flashed into my brain's viewfinder. It made me feel completely weirdo wonky to see him. Totally out of character.

Okay, I admit when Tyler enters my orbit I go

goofy. But Ringo is my total bud. He's like Griffin lite. Our wavelengths work. Except just now I couldn't stand seeing him walk into the room.

"Hi, everybody," he mumbled.

Obviously Ringo felt the same way about me. He couldn't even look at me. How were we going to get past this? It was bad enough that Toni was steamed at me. Life at Trumbull wouldn't be bearable if I couldn't pal around with Ringo.

The problem was, I couldn't meet Ringo's gray eyes. Even my freckles felt self-conscious.

I could only imagine what Ringo was thinking. I mean, when he looked at me, did he picture boobs? Yuck!

Instinctively I crossed my arms over my chest. I didn't want him thinking about that part of me any more than he probably wanted to.

This wasn't fair! How come they had to be pictures of something I had that Ringo didn't? If they were pictures of naked boys, maybe he'd be more embarrassed than me right now.

The tips of his ears poked through his shaggy hair. I could see they were bright red. He was embarrassed enough as it was.

"I . . . uh, I have the cookbook," he said. He placed the cookbook on the table. He leaned against the wall and gazed down at his sneakers.

Okay. One of us had to get the ball rolling

here. Somebody had to be the big one.

Too bad that someone wasn't going to be me. I just couldn't get there.

Neither could Ringo.

"That's great, Ringo," Megan gushed. "I'm sure it will be a big seller for us. We'll make a ton of money."

Gary reached over and picked up the book. Ringo had printed it out and put it into a cool binding with a Simon cartoon on the cover.

Simon Says: Get Cooking!

Gary tipped back in his chair, flipping through the recipes. "This looks good," he complimented Ringo. "Totally professional."

No one seemed to notice that Ringo and I were pretending each other was invisible. Good. Hopefully we would get this worked out before it got really obvious.

"So did you go all veggie?" Toni asked.

"I put in some recipes using chicken . . . I mean some nonvegetarian recipes," Ringo replied, his eyes still looking straight down. His hair fell over his face, so I couldn't see his expression.

"Yeah, and this chicken breast recipe sounds really good," Gary said.

Ringo's eyes flicked at me at the word "breast." This time, *I* glanced down at my sneakers.

"In fact, it's making me hungry," Gary added. "'Chicken Breasts à la Ringo,'" he read. "Mmmmm."

I tried to stifle a giggle. Just hearing the word in front of Ringo made me feel filled with goofy bubbles.

"'Take two chicken breasts,'" Gary continued, reading from the cookbook.

This time a full-blown guffaw burst out of me, followed by a snort, as I tried to keep myself from laughing. I didn't succeed.

I couldn't help it. I was hit with a major case of the giggles.

Everyone stared at me. "Am I missing something?" Gary asked. "Are these supposed to be joke recipes?" He scanned a few pages.

Now Ringo burst out laughing. "No," he said, gasping for breath. "They are totally serious recipes. With serious consequences."

"You guys are whacked," Toni said. She rolled her eyes.

"Did you get into trouble after I left?" Ringo asked, still gulping for air.

"No," I said, wiping my eyes. They'd gone all teary.

"Are you two okay?" Megan asked.

"Get into trouble for what?" Gary demanded. "Cooking without a permit?"

This cracked us up even worse.

"Swear," I gasped. I could tell Ringo knew exactly what I meant. I was asking him to swear that he would never spill what happened.

"To the grave," he promised. He came over, and we linked pinkies. Pinkie swears are irrevocable. "And beyond. Not even if someone asks me with a Ouija board after I'm dead."

Toni hit the table in exasperation. "What is with you two?"

"Nothing," Ringo replied. He forced his face to get serious. I could tell it was a struggle. "What's with you?"

Gary twirled a finger by his temple. *Loco. Mucho loco.*

"I hate to break up this laugh fest," Megan

said, "but I'm baby-sitting this afternoon for the yearbook. I need to get going soon."

Wow. She must be overextended. Yesterday she gave away two great stories. Today she sounded positively irritable.

Megan tapped the eraser end of her pencil on the table. "Okay, if the giggle twins have finished falling apart?"

Ringo and I squeezed our faces into reasonable facsimiles of normal and sat down.

"Thank you," Megan said. "So far we have Casey working on two stories for next week's issue. The Internet scam and Internet issues in general. Both are potential front-pagers."

I beamed. I loved that sentence.

"I'm not sure how your photos will play into this," Megan said to Toni. "Somehow Internet stories don't lend themselves to photos. What do you think?"

"I know!" I burst out. "When I catch the culprit, Toni can be there to cover it! We'll blast that jerk's picture all over the front page."

"Will you please tell the person sitting next to me that that is a totally stupid idea and I won't do it?" Toni said to Ringo.

"Why is it stupid?" I asked her.

Toni turned her back on me. "Ringo," she said. "Please inform this person that I am not speaking

65

to her. I'm also not doing any pictures to go with anything she writes."

Gary, Ringo and Megan looked back and forth between Toni and me. They looked like people watching a tennis match.

"Go ahead, Ringo," Toni said. "Tell her."

Ringo looked uncomfortable. "Uh, Casey, Toni is still feeling a little burned by the e-mail you sent. Because of that, she's not ready for open communication with you."

"That isn't what I said!" Toni exclaimed. "You tell her what I really said or you'll be sorry."

"Casey," Ringo said. "Toni says she doesn't want to take pictures for your stories."

"I know, Ringo," I snapped. "I heard her." I tapped Toni's back. "Toni, I'm sitting right here. You can talk straight to me, please."

Toni snorted and wriggled out from under my finger.

I glared at her back. Fine. Be that way, I thought. You'll change your tune once I catch this culprit. Then you'll be all "Oh, thank you, Casey."

I scrunched my lips together really hard so I wouldn't say any of that out loud. I planned to live to my twelfth birthday.

Tyler darted into the office. "Did I miss anything? Are you talking about catching GoForIt?"

He sat down next to me. "Hey, Toni. I heard you got ripped off too. Bummer."

I winced. I had a feeling Toni didn't want that fact broadcasted.

Toni whirled around. Her fingers gripped the back of her chair so tightly that the olive-toned skin on her knuckles turned white. "It wasn't enough that you dis me in that e-mail," she yelled. "You have to tell the whole school I'm a fool?"

"It wasn't like that," I protested.

"Did I say something wrong?" Tyler asked.

"Ringo," Toni said. "Tell this insect that she is so low that she must live underneath the part of the refrigerator that hums."

"Your refrigerator hums?" Ringo said. "You probably have a loose coil."

"Oh, forget it." Toni popped some more gum into her mouth and chewed loudly.

Tyler leaned in close to me. "Sorry," he whispered in my ear.

I flushed. He was really really close to me. His breath smelled like fruit roll-ups.

Tyler leaned back into his chair. "Let's figure out how to get GoForIt," he said. He was obviously trying to divert Toni from slamming me.

Isn't he perfect?

"This bogus peddler deserves to be exposed and brought down," I declared.

"So how are we going to do that?" Gary asked.

"What do we know so far?" I pulled my notebook from my backpack and took out a pen. I flipped open to a blank page.

"That kid Ben said he did the same thing as Tyler and Toni," I said. "He found the Alienheads on the student bulletin board and sent cash to a post office box."

"Those are clues right there," Tyler said. "Whoever GoForIt is, he—"

"Or she," Ringo pointed out.

Tyler tipped his head toward Ringo in acknowledgment. "Or *she* has access to the student bulletin board. Which means knowing the password. Which means GoForIt is a student at Trumbull."

"Not necessarily," Megan said. "My mom knows the password."

"Yeah," Gary agreed. "It could be a kid who has a friend or brother or something going here. Or even an adult who somehow got the password from a kid."

"Or works here," I added. It was kind of creepy to think someone who worked at the school might cheat kids.

Tyler looked disappointed. "Oh. I guess that wasn't such a big deal clue after all."

"It's a start," I assured him. I made a note:

◆◆◆

Knows password. Kid? Grown-up?

Definitely has some connection to

Trumbull.

I glanced around the table. Toni sneered at me. I ignored her. "What else do we know?"

"The post office box number," Tyler said. "I sent my money to number four-seventeen. That's got to be some kind of clue."

"It's going to be. Toni, was that the same number that you sent your money to?" I asked.

Dead silence.

"Toni?" I repeated.

She looked up at the ceiling.

I realized there was a major flaw in this investigation. One of the prime witnesses wasn't speaking to the investigator.

Fine. I'd just work with her attitude until she had an attitude adjustment.

"Ringo, could you ask Toni what the post office box number was?" I said, way diplomatically.

Toni's behavior was totally immature, but I had a story to get.

"Toni," Ringo began.

"It was the same one," she mumbled.

"Good," I said. "Now we have to figure out which post office that is. That could lead somewhere."

"I brought the address with me," Tyler said. He pulled a crumpled piece of paper from his pocket. He laid it on the table and smoothed it out.

Megan picked it up. "There's a website where I can look up locations by zip code. We can find out if this is local."

"Excellent!"

We all crowded around the computer. Except for Toni. She just sat at the table, her chin resting on the palm of her hand.

I was getting peeved. You'd think she'd care more about the fact that we were all pitching in to solve a problem that affected her. But no. She just sat there all gloomy.

Of course, I'd known Toni long enough to realize that more than anything, Toni hated it if anyone thought she was dumb. Probably because she had some trouble with reading. She has this learning disability, dyslexia, that makes it hard for her to learn to read and write. She was getting a lot better, but it made her kind of sensitive about her smarts.

"The post office is the one right on Main Street," Megan announced.

"So GoForIt lives here in Abbington," I commented. "That's good to know." With the net you never knew where anyone was writing from. We lucked out—GoForIt could have been in England, or on the moon, for all we knew.

"Did GoForIt answer your e-mail?" Megan asked Toni.

"No," Toni replied.

"Big surprise," I muttered.

"What did you say?" Toni demanded.

"I thought you weren't speaking to me," I said. I sat back down and made some more notes. There weren't many. How were we going to go for GoForIt?

Brainstorm! "How about this," I said. "We post a notice on the student bulletin board saying we want to buy an Alienhead and are willing to pay big bucks."

"Good thinking. That way," Tyler said, picking up on my train of thought, "when GoForIt responds, we'll either insist on a face-to-face or scope out that P.O. box."

"Exactly!" Tyler and I slapped high fives.

"It could work," Gary agreed.

"Don't use the e-mail system from *Real News*," Megan said. "Even if GoForIt doesn't notice the address, the signature at the bottom could make him—or her—suspicious."

She was right. Every message sent out from *Real News* had "Keep it real. Read *Real News*" printed across the bottom. That would make GoForIt suspicious instantly.

"I can't send it," I realized. "Everyone at school knows how I feel about Alienheads." Toni snorted. I ignored it. "So GoForIt would never believe I wanted to buy a figurine."

"I'll do it from my home computer," Tyler offered.

"Excellent." I wanted to high-five him again, but since he didn't lift up his hand, I didn't push it.

"Has anyone reported the fraud?" Megan asked. "To anyone? Like the principal? Their parents?"

Gary, Ringo, Megan and I all looked at Tyler. Then at Toni. They both shook their heads no.

I figured that this was good for me, though. I wanted to keep the story under wraps. That way I could be the one to expose the story. A *Real News* exclusive!

I flashed back to my conversation with Principal Nachman. She'd been alerted to the Internet scam. I wondered what that little slip was going to cost me.

"I think we should go down to the post office right now," I said. I wanted to get started.

"I don't know," Megan said. "Are you sure you should go by yourself?"

"I'll go with her," Tyler offered.

How excellent.

CHAPTER
8

Local Kids Go Postal!

TYLER AND I went home to pick up our bikes. Then we met up again and rode over to the post office.

By the time we arrived, it was almost closing time.

We pushed through the doors. "What was the box number again?" I asked Tyler.

"Number four-seventeen," he replied.

One whole wall of the post office was filled with the boxes. We found GoForIt's. It was an ordinary post office box. Metal. Used a key. Between 416 and 418.

Tyler and I stood side by side, staring at box 417.

"What are we looking for?" he whispered.

I shook my head. "I-I'm not sure." I tried to turn the knob. The box was locked. Big surprise.

What did I expect? That GoForIt would jump out of the box and grab us? Or maybe that GoForIt had left it open and scrawled his—or her—phone number and home address on the box?

Get real, I told myself.

"I wish we could take fingerprints," I muttered. Of course they'd be kind of useless. Fingerprints had to be on file somewhere to do you any good. Plus you'd need an expert to read them. Oh well.

Tyler and I hung around, waiting to see if we would get lucky and GoForIt would show up to collect the mail. I could just picture it. GoForIt could walk in, open the box and bingo! Tyler and I would nail him—or her—complete with cash in hand. What a story that would make.

The post office wasn't very busy. The whole time we were there, only one person came in to check a post office box. A little old granny type. Was she GoForIt?

Nope.

Hey—it could happen.

Since the stakeout was turning out to be a total bust, I decided to use the time to get some facts.

"You stay here and watch the box," I instructed Tyler. "I'm going to go ask some questions."

"Sure thing, Commander Casey." Tyler slid

down the wall and sat on the floor. He gave me a thumbs-up. "On the case."

I went up to the information window. A curly-haired man with glasses peered at me.

"Can you tell me about post office boxes?" I asked.

He tipped his head toward Tyler. "They're right over there."

"No, I know. I mean, can anyone buy one?"

"Any adult," the clerk said. "And they're rented, not bought."

"I don't want one," I explained. "I'm just curious how they work."

"Are you doing a report for school, young lady?" the guy asked.

"Uh, yes, sure." That line usually went over with adults. It made them more willing to talk to kids and less suspicious of us.

"So how would a person get a post office box?" I prodded.

"It's easy. We set up an account, and the person pays on a monthly basis."

"Do you keep a list of who owns, I mean, *rents* the boxes?"

"Of course, but we don't give it out. That's private information."

Darn it. That was no help. "Why does someone get a post office box?"

"All sorts of reasons. Often people with home businesses will rent a box so that their home addresses aren't going out to all of their business contacts."

Hm. Selling fake Alienheads could qualify as a home business.

"Some of the boxes are rented by people who are living in temporary situations and don't want their mail service disrupted," the postal clerk continued. "Others live in rural areas with irregular delivery. Sometimes roommates will rent boxes to keep their mail private or because their roommates aren't very responsible and mail goes missing."

"Do people rent them for illegal reasons, too?" I asked.

The man looked sort of surprised. "I suppose it's possible," he admitted. "But using the mail for illegal purposes is a federal offense."

I got even more excited. GoForIt was definitely using the mail for illegal purposes. Selling fake Alienheads was fraud. This was a serious crime! And I intended to catch the criminal.

At least, that was the plan. Too bad GoForIt wasn't cooperating.

No one showed up. The guard finally had to ask us to leave.

Tyler and I unlocked our bikes and rode home.

"Don't worry," he assured me. "We just started. We'll get GoForIt."

"I know." Tyler must have thought I was bumming. He was wrong.

Yeah, it was a drag that we didn't get too far today. But I had that amazing feeling I always get when I'm at the start of a great story. This might turn out to be my biggest so far.

Exhilaration made my feet pump fast, fast, faster! The wind blew my scarf out behind me. I felt as if I was flying. I whipped around the corner.

Whoa! I was going so fast I nearly skidded out. I frantically regained control of the bike.

Don't fall! I ordered myself. I couldn't wipe out in front of Tyler. I wobbled a little, but I was basically upright in a matter of seconds.

Phew. Close call.

Tyler and I split up at our usual spot. As I rode home, I tried to put the pieces of the story together.

Who is GoForIt? I wondered all the way home. That's the weird thing about the Internet. It's so anonymous. I could sit next to GoForIt in homeroom every day and not know it. Or GoForIt could be the school janitor. Or the principal, even!

Nah. Principal Nachman didn't strike me as the type. Besides, the principal probably made a decent salary. She didn't need to rip off kids for twenty bucks. Twenty bucks is a lot of money to a twelve-year-old, though. It might be worth the risk to one of the students. By the looks of things, GoForIt was raking it in. Toni had probably lost almost fifty dollars to GoForIt. I wondered where she had come up with that kind of money.

Well, I certainly wasn't going to ask her. She wasn't speaking to me as it was. Questioning her about where she got her cash would make her go ballistic. Reminding her of how much she lost wouldn't go over too big, either.

I parked my bike and pulled open the front door. Tyler and I wouldn't be able to stake out the post office all day every day. We'd be awfully lucky to catch GoForIt there. I couldn't count on luck. I had to make things happen. But how?

I charged up to my room. First, I figured, I'd see if GoForIt was still selling online. I sat at my desk and logged on.

Wow. My in-box was filled with messages.

I didn't recognize any of the addresses. Maybe they were responses to my research question.

Wait a sec. Didn't I post that from the *Real News* server? So anybody wanting to answer would have replied to that e-mail address. So who were all these messages from?

"More hate mail," I muttered. "Great." I figured the Alienheads defenders found out my home e-mail address or something.

I clicked on to the first message. I gasped out loud. The e-mail was an offer telling me to check out a website that was obviously some kind of porno thing.

I deleted it quickly, and the next message popped onto my screen. This one was even more explicit. I didn't really read it, but I got the gist.

To me, cursing and using bad words is just lazy language skills, so maybe I'm not used to seeing that kind of stuff in print. It was pretty startling.

I deleted it, and another one exactly like it appeared. All of the gross things were addressed personally to me.

That was when I freaked. All of the messages in my in-box must be the same thing. Why were they sending me this gross stuff? More important — how did they get my address?

"Gram!" I called. I hurried downstairs. I knew she was working, but this couldn't wait. I knocked on the door to her study.

"Enter," she called.

I stepped into the room. She wore her red kimono over black leggings and T-shirt, her writing uniform. She didn't look up from the computer.

"Gram—" I began. Her back was to me, but she held up a hand to stop me from speaking. She typed a few words, then turned around.

"Sorry, I was afraid I'd lose my train of thought. I'd finally figured out how to say what I had been trying to say all morning. But now you have my undivided attention."

"There's weird stuff on my computer," I blurted.

Her brow crinkled. "Weird in what way? Is the system crashing?"

"No, I mean, I got really creepy e-mail."

"From whom?" she asked. Concern now spread across her face.

"I don't know," I replied. "I don't understand how they have my e-mail address."

She stood up and draped her arm across my shoulders. She gave me a squeeze. "Let's go take care of this right now."

We went back up to my room. I perched at the foot of my bed. She sat down at my desk and checked the e-mail. "Hm. I have a feeling your little recipe search resulted in these."

Huh? How could that be? "What do you mean?" I asked. "How?"

She turned around in the chair to face me. "You visited an adult site. The computer doesn't know you went there by accident. These sites probably use cookies."

"Cookies?" Food had never caused me so

many problems before. First chicken breasts got me all embarrassed, and now cookies were sending me gross e-mail.

"You know that the way the Internet works is by having computers talking to each other, right?"

I nodded. "That other computer needs to have its mouth washed out with soap."

Gram laughed. "You're right."

"How did their computer start talking to mine?" I asked.

"I'm not completely sure," Gram replied. "Did you personalize your homepage?"

"Yes." I fixed it so I got different news services and the TV schedule when I logged on.

"That may have something to do with it," Gram said. "Your browser and your service provider are integrated. When you configured your homepage you probably automatically set up some cookies. Cookies are code in a computer that remembers things about you. So when you accidentally went to those sites, their cookie file checked to see if you had cookies in your computer. Your e-mail address was probably in one of those files. These sites found the address there and are now sending you mail."

"I don't want them to! I want them to stop!" I glared in the direction of the computer.

"It's not going to be that easy. Unfortunately."

My heart sank. One stupid mistake, and now I had to jump through hoops to stop it?

Gram drummed her fingers on the table. "There are a few different ways to approach this. The first thing we'll do is report it to your Internet service provider. I have to decide whether or not I should send a message to the different sites. After all, soliciting minors to view adult material is illegal."

"Why wouldn't you just do that?" I asked.

"Responding to these addresses may not actually get any results—it's possible no one reads the messages. And it could result in your getting even more mail."

"Oh," I said. "I don't want that."

"Another thing to do is use filters."

"You can do that?" I got up and stood by her chair and stared at the computer. Luckily Gram had closed the e-mail. Nothing there but the desktop.

She nodded. "Most Internet providers have parental controls available. Just like we were talking about yesterday."

"How would that work?"

"We could either list all of these addresses as e-mail sources to block, which would take time and allow some new ones to fall through the cracks. Or we could set it up so that the only e-mails you can receive are from specified addresses. Anything else would be blocked."

"But I never know who I'm going to hear from," I protested. "I get new mail all the time." This was really frustrating.

Gram nodded. "Then that isn't the way to go. Okay, we'll set up blocks against these specific addresses. You might get a few more, but as long as you don't open them they should stop after a while. And I'll contact your provider and alert them to what has happened. They may have some other suggestions."

I stared at my computer. I've always loved the Internet—the way it opens up the whole world to me right here in my room. That world suddenly seemed a lot scarier and more dangerous than I realized. And now blocking software and filters made sense to me.

All of those safety lessons hit home. Not just as hypotheticals, but on the reality plane. What if I had given those creeps my home address? My last name? It was bad enough that they were coming after the *virtual* me.

Visiting those sites had consequences. Not as dangerous as in the real world, of course. But creepy to the max.

While Gram dealt with the junk e-mail, I sat on

my bed thinking about all this Internet stuff. I'd always taken it all for granted. But now with this, and the Alienheads scam, well, it changed my view of the information superhighway. As if I'd suddenly discovered potholes and weird off-ramps that led to deadends and down dark alleyways.

If I was going to catch GoForIt, I was going to have to learn a lot more about the dark side of the web. Just like those creeps tracked me, I'd have to figure out a way to track GoForIt.

Actually, I was going to have to learn a lot more about the web, period. I never concerned myself with how any of it worked, just how I could use it for what I needed it for: homework, research, and writing to my friends.

Then it hit me. I knew exactly who might have some answers. Wheelies. There was even a tech-help site on the web page. Serious netheads were at my fingertips.

"That should take care of that," Gram declared. She stood up and stretched. "All that inputting made me hungry. I've got a craving for Chinese food. Sound okay?"

"Yum," I replied. "Uh, Gram, I'm sorry I caused all these problems."

"No apology necessary, chick-a-doodle. Let me know if anything else happens."

"Believe me, I will," I promised.

Gram headed downstairs to phone our favorite take-out place. I went to the computer and sent Wheelies an e-mail.

To: Wheelies
From: Wordpainter
Re: Need some info!
　　Hi! My name is Casey Smith, and I write for *Real News*. We're doing a couple of stories about the Internet, and could definitely use your computer savvy. Would you be able to drop by the office tomorrow after classes? We're down in the basement near the boiler room.
　　Thanks,
　　Casey
　　P.S. Wheelies's Web World rocks!

Wheelies must have been online. Just a few minutes later I received a reply.

I'm there!

I grinned at the screen. I felt good. It takes a big person to know when she needs help, I congratulated myself. I did the right thing, calling in a specialist. A consultant. Besides, it will be fun having an F2F with the person behind the web page.

I knew Gram didn't want me meeting anyone I met online without her, but I figured I would be safe at school. I would just make sure the whole *Real News* gang was with me.

I logged off. I wished there was more I could do to work on the story. I needed to catch GoForIt before the Thursday deadline if I wanted to get the story into next week's issue. I hated waiting around for things to happen. It is so not me.

I jumped up and went to the phone. Maybe GoForIt had responded to Tyler's bait.

I tucked a strand of straight brown hair behind my ear, and dialed Tyler's number. I bounced a little on my toes while I listened to the ring. Someone on the other end picked up the receiver. My heart thudded a little harder. A little faster.

"Hello," a voice said.

Tyler's dad. I let out the breath I'd been holding. "Hi, Mr. Mackenzie. This is . . . um . . . Casey? You know, Smith. Casey Smith?"

What was wrong with me? I sounded as if I didn't know my own name.

I took in a breath. "IsTylerthere?" I said in a rush.

"No, Casey, I'm sorry. He's gone with his mom to run errands."

Dead silence. Oh, right. It was my turn to speak.

"Uh, so, okay," I mumbled.

"Do you want Tyler to call you when he gets in?"

"He doesn't have to. That's okay." I put down the receiver.

Oops. I basically hung up on Tyler's dad.

Darn it. I shouldn't have called. Now Tyler's dad thought I was calling a boy. Well, I was, but not that way. To make it worse, I had just made a complete fool of myself. What was Mr. McKenzie going to tell Tyler? "Oh, that dorky dodo from Trumbull called. The writer who got me fired. Hard to believe she's a writer. She barely seems capable of using words."

My first column for *Real News* had been about how Riverhead Paper Mill was polluting the Sussex River. The good news was that the mill was shut down, the pollution was stopped. The bad news—Tyler's dad lost his job at the mill.

I slumped into my desk chair and covered my face with my hands. Stupid, stupid, stupid. Then I sat up straight. Hold on, I told myself. I had a valid excuse—I mean *reason*—to call Tyler. Catching a criminal was totally legit.

That was my story, and I was sticking to it.

CHAPTER 9

Color Coordination Counters Klutzy Conversation!

TYLER NEVER DID call me back. The next morning I still obsessed a little over what Tyler's dad might have said to him. How stupid had I sounded?

I took extra care in matching my purple Converse sneakers to my purple socks. I knew I'd be seeing Tyler today. After all, he was part of this investigation.

My favorite purple turtleneck was in the laundry, so I compromised with a blue one. It wasn't that I cared about how I looked or anything. I needed to appear on the ball. Especially if Tyler's dad let it slip that I was a phone failure.

"Have you checked your e-mail this morning?" Gram asked as she poured me some OJ.

"Yup. All clear." I held up my hand and showed her my crossed fingers. "I hope it stays that way."

"Let me know if anything else happens," Gram said.

I took a bite of toast. "One good thing came out of it," I remarked. "I got excellent material for my story about Internet issues."

Gram sipped some coffee and smiled. "You are a true reporter, kiddo. You find the story angle in everything."

At school I went to the *Real News* office before homeroom. I had all that I needed for the Internet safety issues story. I had spoken to representatives of a few of the makers of blocking software and talked with my own Internet provider about controls.

The software makers took the position that they were actually protecting the First Amendment. "By putting the choices in the hands of the parents," the public relations lady at CyberSafe told me, "we don't have to regulate the Net. Free speech will flourish on the Internet itself, but not at the expense of the safety of children or the interests of parents."

Sounds good, right? Only there's one problem. A lot of the software and blocking controls made by Internet providers don't tell you who they block or why. So some companies have gotten into trouble because they block sites with political points of view or standards that are different from their own. Some block access to things that may include information on birth control or gay rights or gun control because they disagree with the content.

There are a few reasons they don't disclose the sites. One could be because they don't want the buyer to know the political agenda behind the software makers. Another is plain old money— they don't want their competitors to know who they block.

Of course, after my recent experience with unwanted e-mail, I could understand the usefulness of blocks. That mail had been triggered by an accidental visit to an adult site. If those filters or blocks had already been in place, the only thing that would have come up when Ringo and I typed in "chicken breasts" would have been recipes.

Or nothing at all.

The software can't be all that specific. I thought back to the system in the library that wouldn't allow us to access anything. I wondered how much information I wasn't getting when I did research at school.

Which led me right back to thinking that blocking software was a violation of the First Amendment and interfered with every citizen's right to access to information. Whatever that information might be.

The software program that really freaked me out was the kind that lets people know what sites have been visited. Talk about Big Brother! A parent or a school librarian can check a file to see who has been going where online. That just struck me as plain old wrong.

But then there was that tricky flip side. Some troubled kids might have been reached sooner if their parents had known about the kinds of freaky sites they'd been visiting. Sites where they learned how to make bombs or sites that fueled prejudice and stuff.

My poll got some interesting results, too. I had expected kids to be totally against blocking software, but it didn't go that way.

"I don't mind that my parents have set the guidelines in the computer," one kid wrote. "I wouldn't want to go to those sites anyway."

"I always check with my parents before I submit forms with personal information. That's the deal we have. So right now, there aren't any controls. I don't really know if that would matter."

"Sometimes it annoys me when I do a search and I'm blocked for no good reason. But I just tell my dad what I'm looking for, and he'll do a search on his computer."

There were a few on the other side:

"It makes me mad that my parents don't trust me."

"Anything that interferes with our rights of free speech is totally bogus!"

"My older brother is bugged by the sites our parents have blocked. But he goes to his friend's house and plays those games there. I don't know what the big deal is myself."

No one seemed to think they had been affected in any harmful way. That was certainly true—at least on the surface. Who knows what additional useful information they might have found if there weren't any blocks?

On the other hand, there is a lot of junk on the net. Ridiculous stories sent out as truth, rumors, hate sites, sites on how to make poison or bombs. Creepo stuff.

At least Megan would like this story, I thought. I was really working both sides of the issue. She couldn't complain that I was just going off on a rant. Especially since I wasn't exactly sure where I fell on the issue. There I was, stuck in the middle of that tricky gray area.

I wondered how Wheelies felt about all this. From the website, I figured Wheelies would be totally against censorship in any form.

For my story, I decided to just lay out the

facts. My final point was that the Internet is new enough that everybody is still trying to figure it out. Individuals have to decide for themselves. The blocking software is out there, but no one is forcing anyone to install it. For now. That leaves the choice in our hands. Where it should be.

One story down. On to the next. I had to nail GoForIt fast to come up with the front-pager.

Hopefully, Wheelies would help me do just that.

Megan came into the office. She looked stressed. Two whole strands of blond hair were actually out of place. "Hi, Casey," she greeted me. To my shock, her glitter barrettes did not match her outfit.

She *must* be tired.

"I have to get my 'JAM' column finished," she explained. "This is the only chance I'll have today. I have extra chores after school."

"I'm sick of hearing about your precious yearbook fund-raiser," I complained. "You still haven't contributed anything to the *Real News* auction, and there's only one week left to go. Don't you care that *Real News* is at the bottom of the fund-raising heap?"

"Of course I care," she snapped. "Why do you always do that?"

"Do what?" I asked.

"Accuse people of not caring, just because they don't act like you do."

That caught me up short. It sounded like something Gary and Toni had both said to me recently. "I don't do that," I protested. "If you *act* like you don't care, all I can do is assume that you *don't.*"

Megan sighed. She just didn't have the energy to fight with me. "I really thought the auction idea was a good one," she said. "We all did. I don't know why it's a bust."

"Because we haven't all contributed," I said pointedly. Okay, so maybe I was kicking her when she was down, but this was important, and it seemed as if I was the only one who realized that.

"Maybe we should add chores to what the kids can bid on," she suggested. "Chores sold really well for the yearbook."

Great idea. Only one major problem. "Who will do the chores, Megan?" I demanded. "You're already overextended. Gary has a gazillion sports events to cover. Toni isn't exactly a team player, in case you haven't noticed." I put my hands on my hips. "So gee, who would be the people to actually *do* those chores? The way I figure, it would be up to Ringo and me. And we've both already contributed. It's totally not fair!"

"I'm sorry, I'm sorry. It was just an idea," Megan said. "I was just thinking out loud."

Megan pulled out a folder and began poring over her 'JAM' letters. I did one last check of the bids on Gram's book.

Someone upped my bid! I wanted to get up and do a little happy dance, but I'd have Megan as a witness.

I glanced over at Megan. She was totally engrossed in her 'JAM' column. I quickly raised the bid on Gram's book. If someone was interested in it for real, surely they'd top my bid. I'd known her book would be a success! And they had doubted me. I'd show them.

"See you later," I told Megan. "I already wrote up the Internet issues story. One down, one to go. See how on top of things I am?"

I couldn't help it. I wanted to rub it in. Usually she was the one hounding me to get better organized. Ms. Goody-goody was finally slipping down the perfection scale.

I ran into Tyler in the hallway. "Hi, Casey. My dad told me you called."

I immediately went to my cover story. "I wanted to see if you heard from GoForIt yet," I told him.

He totally bought it. "Negativo, agent Casey.

But I have high hopes."

The bell rang, so we split up to head to our homerooms. "Check in with you later," he called over his shoulder.

After attendance was taken, Principal Nachman's voice came over the loudspeaker. "It has come to my attention that there have been some unfortunate incidents involving sales over the student bulletin board. This is not what the bulletin board was intended for. From now on, there will be no sales at all through the bulletin board. To insure compliance, there will be periodic checks. If anyone abuses the bulletin board, all students will lose. It will no longer be available. This will not affect the *Real News* auction, however. That may continue, because it is properly monitored."

The loudspeaker crackled, and the message was over.

So was our plan to catch GoForIt.

What lousy timing! Now how were we going to run our sting? We couldn't catch GoForIt without bait. We didn't have the first clue about GoForIt's identity. Without the student bulletin board, we had no way to get to him.

Our only hope was serious computer whizzing from Wheelies. I hoped Wheelies was up to it.

At lunch, I couldn't stop scoping out all the kids

in the cafeteria. Could one of them be GoForIt? What's the profile of an Internet scammer?

PROFILE OF INTERNET SCAMMER
Internet access—could be anyone!!! Can log on at school, at home, at libraries, at cybercafes, at friends' houses.
P.O. Box access—Has to be a grown-up to rent one.
Is GoForIt an adult? Or a kid who can get into their parents' mailbox?
Password access—tricky. Linked somehow to Trumbull. A student? Former student? Parent of a student. Whoever they are—they know Trumbull.

I added some personality traits, too.

No problem cheating kids—if this is a grown-up then they are MEAN!
Kid might be more likely. A grown-up might cheat at a higher dollar level.

Arrogant—"GoForIt" is practically a
scammer's dare!

I thought of some other things to look for:

Fake Alienheads to unload—where'd
GoForIt get them from anyway?
Sudden cash—who do we know has
some? Anyone spending lots of dough
recently??

Aaarrrgghhh! Who could GoForIt be?
After classes, I raced to the *Real News* office.
It was empty.
"Come on, people," I muttered. "We've got a
crook to catch."
Unfortunately, Toni was the first person to
arrive. She was still icing me out.
This is getting ridiculous, I thought, as she
carefully chose a chair that would let her sit with
her back to me.
By the time the rest of the *Real News* staff—
and Tyler—filed in, I was practically bouncing
off the walls. Once they had all plunked down
around the table, I made my announcement.

"I've called in reinforcements," I declared. "I've asked a computer expert to help us track this Internet thief."

"That was smart," Megan said. "Who is your expert?"

"Have you ever checked out Wheelies's Web World?" I asked.

"That Nethead site?" Gary asked.

"Wheelies is awesome," Toni argued. "Just because it doesn't include sports stats, that doesn't make it geeky."

Toni might not be talking to me, but at least she was scoring points for my side.

"I like Wheelies, too," Ringo said. "Did you read the 'Gripes' column about ever-changing TV schedules? Wheelies got it right. How can we watch our favorite shows if we can never figure out what day or time they're on?"

"Well, Wheelies has agreed to act as our Internet advisor," I said.

"Did someone mention my name?"

All heads whipped to the doorway.

All mouths dropped open.

"What?" the girl in the wheelchair demanded. "Haven't you ever seen a polka-dot laptop before?"

CHAPTER 10

Popping Wheelies Works Wonders!

I DIDN'T KNOW where to look. I was afraid that if I looked at the girl I'd stare. But if I looked away it would seem weird. Either way, I'd be rude.

I'd seen her around, of course. How could you miss her? She was the only person at Trumbull in a wheelchair.

Her name was Shannon or Sharon—something like that. She was a seventh grader, so we never really crossed paths except in the halls sometimes. I had heard all sorts of different reasons why she was in a wheelchair, but none of them sounded very believable. Like she had been an Olympic horse jumper and had an accident, or had ordinary surgery but it went horribly wrong. Stuff along those lines. Typical middle-school rumors.

Gary sometimes complained about standing out because he was one of the few African-American kids at school. Well, he had nothing on Wheelies. I wondered if that bothered her.

Toni recovered first. "Wheelies. I get it. Awesome screen name. Mine's HotStuff. In the reality plane, I'm Toni."

A look of recognition crossed Wheelies's face. "I've seen you post in the chat room sometimes," Wheelies said. "I totally agree that Badboy was out of line in that flame."

"Thanks," Toni said. "Badboy knows he better not mess with HotStuff again."

The girl wheeled deeper into the room. "Which one of you is Casey?' she asked.

"I . . . that . . . I mean, that's me," I stammered.

I noticed the girl's head sat on her neck sort of crooked, as if she had trouble holding it up straight. All I kept thinking was, What is wrong with her? Is she sick? Is it contagious? Did she have an accident? Is she going to spend her whole life in a wheelchair, or is this temporary?

Because all those questions were going through my head, nothing was coming out of my mouth.

"My real name is Shannon Butler. I just use Wheelies online."

"I can understand," I said. I cringed when I

heard myself. What did that mean? *I can understand.* The girl must think I'm a total idiot.

"Welcome to *Real News,* Shannon," Megan said brightly. In fact, she sounded downright chirpy. More so than usual. She smiled broadly.

I was surprised. Megan seemed a little nervous. I had pegged Megan to be one of those natural hostess types. Instead, her peppiness seemed strained. "Please join us."

"Are you the tour guide?" Shannon asked Megan. "As far as I can tell, I've had the whole tour. This room is it, right?"

Megan looked flustered. "I just meant—"

"That's okay, I'm just playing with you." She gazed around the room. I noticed it was hard for her to turn her head. She sighed. "Okay. Let's get this over with. Yes. You're seeing right. I'm in a wheelchair. I have been since I could sit up."

"So what's the deal?" Toni asked.

I was stunned. And I've been accused of being too blunt.

The question didn't seem to bother Shannon, though. "I have cerebral palsy. When I was born there was some damage to my brain. Basically, it means there are certain things I can't do. Like use my legs. My brain just doesn't get the message through to those muscles."

She seemed so up front about it. As if it was

nothing. Even though she explained what was wrong with her, I still felt a little weird around her.

"So, Casey, you said you needed web advice."

"Yes, Shannon," I said. I hated how stiff and formal I sounded. "We have this problem, and we were hoping you would help us with your expertise."

"Bring it on," she said. "I'm game."

I laid out the whole situation for her. I was stunned when Toni admitted to Shannon that she was one of GoForIt's victims.

"You all must be newbies," Shannon commented. "You fell for some pretty obvious stuff."

Toni's eyes narrowed. "I don't remember asking for your opinion," she snapped. "We just want to know from you how to catch GoForIt."

Shannon seemed totally unfazed. "Whatever. Do you still have GoForIt's e-mail address?"

"I do." Tyler pulled a piece of paper from his pocket. He brought it over to Shannon.

"We're in luck. GoForIt uses the same ISP as me. That might make this easy."

"ISP?" I asked.

"Internet service provider," Shannon explained. "You know, who I get my e-mail account from and all that jazz."

"Why will that help?" Megan asked.

"The first thing I'm going to do is put GoForIt

on my buddy list. That will tell me if he's online. I'll also look in the member's profile and see if there is a listing for GoForIt. There are some other directories I can check as well, but they aren't local. We could find a GoForIt in Hawaii in there and that wouldn't do us much good."

"Don't you have to plug into a phone or something?" Ringo asked.

"I have a wireless connection," Shannon explained. "It isn't always convenient for me to try to find a phone jack to plug into."

"Then it is a very good thing that you have wireless," I said. Eww. I sounded all forced and awkward.

Gary stood up and grabbed his backpack. "Now that Shannon has the investigation under control, I've got to book. Game to cover."

"It's still *my* investigation," I reminded him. "Shannon is just consulting. If you had stories that required thinking, you'd need a consultant from day one."

"Tell yourself that if it makes you feel better," he said as he left the room.

I gritted my teeth. Why did he have to dis me in front of Shannon? I turned around to see her reaction, but she was engrossed in what she was doing on the computer.

It was weird to watch Shannon work on her

laptop. Her hands were curved in a sort of awkward way, but she still managed to fly across those keys.

"Hey, your laptop matches our table," Ringo said. "Like it was karma that you work with *Real News.*"

Shannon grinned. "Our dots were calling out to each other," she joked. "Little did I know when I stuck all those stickers on my laptop that I'd be sending signals down to the basement."

"Dot's right," Ringo replied with a grin.

"Well, so far I'm not having any luck," Shannon reported. "GoForIt's real name isn't here in the members directory. Hm. Not in this one either. Obviously our little scammer wants to stay anonymous."

"I can see why," Tyler said.

"That's all right, Shannon," I assured her. "I'm sure you'll find us something." What was with my voice? I sounded all syrupy, like a kindergarten teacher.

She gave me one of those "duh" expressions. "I wasn't worried."

Yowch. Maybe I should just keep my mouth shut until I could sound human. Or at least less like Megan.

Shannon squinted and pursed her lips. She looked deep in thought. "GoForIt. GoForIt," she murmured. "That screen name sounds familiar," she said. "I think I've seen it in the chat room."

"That could be a clue," Tyler said. "GoForIt is probably a kid, if he's posting to KidSpeak."

I remembered what Gram had told me, that sometimes weird adults lurked on kid sites. "Not necessarily," I pointed out. "But it's a start," I added quickly. I didn't want Tyler to feel slighted, and I didn't want Shannon to think I just liked to toss cold water on other people's ideas.

"I'll keep my eye out for GoForIt. Kids reveal all sorts of personal info without realizing it in chat rooms," Shannon said.

"Do you keep transcripts of the chats?" Megan asked. "We might be able to find that personal info there."

I wish I had thought of that. For some reason, Shannon's condition had me distracted. I wasn't on the ball. Focus, Casey, I ordered myself. This is YOUR story. So far, everyone has been contributing ideas except you.

"Can you cookie GoForIt from your website?" I asked. There. I finally sounded as if I knew something.

"I don't record transcripts, but I do have a log that enters visitors' names. I also have a file where I sometimes make notes about repeat visitors."

"How did you get so good on the computer?" Toni asked.

"I've been using a computer since I was really little," Shannon explained. "It was one of the reasons why I was able to be in regular school. I have trouble gripping a pencil, but I can write with the keyboard. See—the keys are extra big. That helps me avoid typing mistakes."

Wow. School was hard enough some days without adding on extra tasks. How hard would if be if I couldn't do the basics—like holding a pencil?

I slid my hands under my butt. I suddenly felt self-conscious about having working fingers. Was Shannon jealous of kids who were . . . well . . . normal?

Shannon's eyes flicked back to the screen. "Well, well, well. Guess who just logged on."

"GoForIt?" Toni said. "Let me at him!" Toni actually climbed over the table to get to Shannon. "Where is the creep?"

Shannon wheeled herself a few inches backward. "Slow down, HotStuff," she said. "We don't want to scare him off." She gave Toni a skeptical look. "And right now, you're scaring *me*."

"Sorry," Toni muttered. She slid back onto the table. "What did GoForIt log on to?"

"I'm not sure. But let me check KidSpeak." Shannon clicked a few keys. "I knew it was the same dude."

"What do you mean?" Tyler asked.

"Some people always use signatures or typical sign-offs. GoForIt always signs his stuff 'Till the next time . . .'"

"So go get him," Toni urged.

"Tell him you want to buy some Alienheads," I said. "If you think that's a good idea," I added.

Again with the Meganitis! If I kept this up, I'd end up wearing pink ruffles. What was wrong with me?

"I'll instant-message him," Shannon said.

Tyler stood behind Shannon's wheelchair and read from her screen. "'Dear GoForIt, I hear you have awesome Alienheads for sale. I'm looking to buy. Can we hook up?'"

Shannon hit Send. Everyone in the room stared at Shannon's computer. Shannon started to laugh. "People," she said. "If you all don't start breathing, I'll have to call nine-one-one. And I'm not so great at dialing regular phones."

I was stunned. She could actually make jokes about her condition.

"Go for the bait, GoForIt," Toni murmured.

"Go for it, GoForIt," Tyler said.

Ringo jumped up into the air with a whoop and did an antigravity split. "Go for it, GoForIt! GoForIt! Go for it, GoForIt!" he chanted.

We all joined in. "GoForIt! GoForIt! Go for it,

GoForIt!" we cheered. Toni beat her hands on the table in time with our chant, while Ringo and I clapped. Tyler stomped his feet. Megan stared at us, and Shannon laughed.

"You people need to get out more," she joked.

Megan packed up her stuff. "Listen, I'm really sorry, but I have to go. Let me know what happens. It was really nice of you to help us, Shannon."

Ringo glanced up at the clock. "Oh no! I went into a major time warp. The rest of the cheerleaders are going to flip."

"Isn't that what they're supposed to do?" Shannon said with a sly grin.

Ringo looked puzzled, then his face brightened and he laughed. "You're right. Maybe my lateness will inspire them to major new moves. Later, all." He dashed out of the room.

"Actually I've gotta book, too," Shannon said. "Maureen goes psycho if I'm late."

"Who's Maureen?" Toni asked.

"My PT," Shannon replied. "Physical therapist," she explained when she caught our blank expressions. "And when I'm late, she insists I do the flips. And they sure aren't my strong suit."

I gaped at her.

She rolled her eyes. "Kidding, Casey. Sheesh. Lighten up. I'll let you know the minute I hear from GoForIt." She wheeled out of the room.

"Way to go all dorky," Toni taunted. "What was with you?"

"Oh, I see. *Now* you're speaking to me," I snapped.

"Somebody has to," she said. "You almost blew it with Shannon. Then where would you be on this case?"

"What are you talking about?" I demanded. I hated that Tyler was watching this fight, but Toni started it. I had to defend myself. "I didn't almost blow anything. I brought her in, remember?"

"You made her all uncomfortable," Toni said.

"I did not!" It was more the other way around, but I didn't say that.

"Shannon didn't seem uncomfortable at all," Tyler countered

Wow. Tyler was standing up for me. Serious coolness. Not that I wanted him to fight my battles or anything. It was just nice to know that he was on my side.

"Whatever." Toni left.

Tyler and I walked out of the building. He was heading over to the mall. He asked me if I wanted to go with him, but I felt too weird inside. I needed to work out this Shannon thing. I didn't want to talk about it with Tyler because I was afraid he would think less of me if he knew how uncomfortable I had felt around her.

Am I a bad person? I wondered as I trudged up the walk to my house. I didn't *think* I was. Mouthy, okay. Sometimes overly direct, maybe. Sarcastic, for sure. But bad?

I knew someone who would tell me the flat-out bald-eyed truth. Griffin. I owed him an e-mail anyway. Every time I had started to write to him, something loopy would distract me. Like wacko e-mail.

To: Thebeast
From: Wordpainter
Re: Long time no e

Sorry it's been a while. Things have been pretty freaky here. I haven't been venturing much into cyberspace.

I filled him in on what happened with Ringo, and with the gross-out spam e-mail. Then I got around to my main event.

The story I'm working on for Real News required an expert so I asked this person I knew from a school site. When she came in, my brain (or something) went out the window.

I explained about Shannon and how I went all wonky.

I was bending over backwards trying to be nice and stuff. So then Toni accuses <u>me</u> of making Shannon uncomfortable.

The thing was—and you are the ONLY person I can say this to—it was <u>so</u> the other way around. I couldn't look at her without feeling weird. I didn't know how to talk to her. I kept wondering if she was jealous that we were healthy. If she was in pain. It was totally distracting, so normal conversation went AWOL. The weird thing was, I had thought Wheelies and I would have a lot in common.

Do you think I'm a terrible person? I don't think I'm prejudiced against her or anything. I admit I was kind of wigged.

I waited for Griffin to respond. I hoped he was online. I didn't want to wait too long for an answer to this question.

Fate smiled down upon me. That had to be a good sign.

To: Wordpainter
From: Thebeast
Re: Hate to tell you, but you're NORMAL

You have had SOME week! Leave you alone in cyberspace and all sorts of things happen. Nothing this interesting ever happens to me!

On the Shannon/Wheelies front: Quit beating yourself up. You were thrown by seriously new information. Maybe once the shock wears off, your brain will return.

Here's what I would do: I'd check out all I could on cerebral palsy. The more you know, the more you'll understand what's up. She's not any different now that you met her in person. A lot of times people don't seem to match their screen name. Well, yours does, but not everyone's. That gap between real and virtual is a toughie. But I bet you and Wheelies/Shannon still have plenty in common.

BTW, my parents have that blocking software you talked about. So I guess if I ever need a recipe for chicken breasts, I know who to turn to.

I smiled at the screen. Of course Griffin was right. When in doubt—research! Why didn't I think of that? Duh. Because I wasn't operating with all burners.

I typed in a search for "cerebral palsy."

Wow. A ton of sites popped up. Before I could open any up, I got an instant message from Shannon.

To: Wordpainter
From: Wheelies
Re: Bad news
   Hate to tell you, but the baddie is onto us. GoForIt has changed his e-mail profile and configuration. All messages to GoForIt have been returned as undeliverable.

Oh no. There went Plan B. And we didn't have a Plan C.

Story Vanishes Without a Trace!

I HATED GoForIt for doing this! I quickly typed a reply to Wheelies.

To: Wheelies
From: Wordpainter
Re: That's worse than bad news—it's a disaster!
    Now what are we going to do? We have no way to catch GoForIt, which means no front-page story! I don't have a backup.
    Any suggestions?

I hit Send and then got up and paced around the room. I didn't have Wheelies on my own buddy list, so I couldn't IM her. It could take a while before she realized she had a message from me.

Think, I ordered myself. You have to get this story! How else can we go after GoForIt?

Pacing wasn't working for me. I sat back down at the computer. Excellent. Shannon had already written back.

I wasn't so thrilled once I read her message.

To: Wordpainter
From: Wheelies
Re: Unbelievable!

You really are something. I don't think I've met anyone so self-centered. All you care about is your story. What about the kids who got ripped off? I thought THAT was the point—to get their money back and keep new kids from getting cheated.

Get your priorities straight, and then maybe we can work on this together.

Steam blasted out of my ears. She didn't know me at all. Of course, I cared about the rip-offs! That's why I wanted to write the story—to bring the scam out into the open and alert people. That's the point of journalism—to inform, reveal.

Okay, so it's also about the byline, but that is so secondary.

My fingers hovered over the keyboard, ready to zing her. Only here's what I typed instead.

To: Wheelies
From: Wordpainter
Re: You're right
    I'm sorry. You're totally right.
    So what's next?

I hit Send and gazed blankly at the computer screen. Why didn't I slam her? If Megan, or Gary or even Toni had sent that message I'd have flattened them, no prob. I just couldn't bring myself to go after Shannon.

To: Wordpainter
From: Wheelies
Re: Probation
    Fine. I'll help until you blow it again.
    I checked the student bb, and Toni posted a warning about GoForIt. So we know the why behind the name change. Here's my suggestion: Go to KidSpeak and see if someone shows up signing off with "Till the next time." I'll keep an eye on Wheelies's Web World and see if anyone signs on that could be GoForIt. Until we figure out this creep's new handle, we'll get no place.

No place. Just where I didn't want to be. I didn't much want to be in a chat room either, but it didn't look as if I had a choice. I sent a reply to Wheelies saying "A-OK, boss" and then clicked into KidSpeak.

I don't get the appeal of chat rooms. Going into a private chat with your friends is one thing—instant conference call. But to sit in front of your computer typing sentences that were supposed to pass as conversation with a group of strangers? No thanks. Most of what I've seen tends to be lame jokes, bathroom humor and flaming. It seems to all be about topping each other, not having an actual conversation. Basically whoever types fastest gets to say the most. It did improve my typing skills, though. I had to admit that.

I lurked in KidSpeak for a while. The usual comments about what TV show ruled, and what movies were bogus. Some goofball jokes that were *so* not funny. Zingers launched against each other.

How can anyone spend time here? I wondered. What a waste. I like my pals live, not virtual.

Hm. Except for Shannon. For some reason, I was far more comfortable dealing with her over the net. Okay, not for *some* reason. There was a very obvious reason. I had trouble having a face-to-face interface with her. The wheelchair thing put me off. I couldn't stand myself for thinking that, but there it was.

Griff was right. I needed to focus on Shannon, not on her condition. And the more I knew, the less weird it would seem. As soon as I was done staking out KidSpeak, I'd do some research.

The conversation on the screen seemed to be mostly between some kids called Worm, awesome123, and Aces. There were other kids online, but those three dominated. They weren't saying anything very interesting. Aces told awesome123 that Alienheads was going to be out on DVD before video. Wow. What a newsflash. Awesome123 complained about not having a DVD player, and Worm bragged s/he had all the technology anyone might ever want. I wondered how much exaggeration was going on in there.

Then my eyes widened. Aces was signing off— using the phrase "Till the next time."

Bingo. I just figured out GoForIt's new screen name.

At least I can stop hanging in KidSpeak, I thought. I logged out and pulled up the earlier search I had done on cerebral palsy.

It was intense. I pored over document after document. "Cerebral palsy" was a big term, covering a whole range of problems. The one thing it always meant: that the brain had been damaged before birth, during birth, or in the first few years after birth. It was an injury, not a disease.

I discovered there were lots of different types of injuries that fell under the umbrella of cerebral palsy. It depended on what part of the brain had been affected and how severely. What they all shared was the fact that the brain was damaged in such a way that it interfered with the brain's ability to send messages to the muscles and nerves. In some people, one side of the body was affected, or just the body from the waist down. Some people had seizures, or were blind; others were mentally retarded. There were articles about illnesses related to cerebral palsy—breathing problems, for example, because of the lack of movement. It was over-whelming. According to one study, approximately 500,000 people in this country have some degree of cerebral palsy.

As I read more, though, I found it really inter-esting how much kids with this problem still could do. Obviously not the worst-case scen-arios, but kids like Shannon, who, from what I could tell, had something called diplegia, which meant the injury had only affected the part of the brain that controlled her legs. Kids with diplegia might also have some problems with their upper bodies, but it was usually not so severe that it interfered with normal functioning. She didn't seem to have the other problems, like vision or hearing impairment. I didn't know if she had seizures, which affect about half the kids with cerebral palsy.

I had admired Wheelies because of how savvy and clever she was. Now I admired Shannon for being such a regular kid, despite the problems she faced every day. I wondered about her family. Did she have brothers or sisters? One of the articles I read talked about how important it was to not be overprotective and to let your kid have as normal a life as possible. Shannon was in a regular school, doing regular things.

It must be so hard, though. No matter how much like a regular kid Shannon behaved, she was still different, and different in a way that would never change. I still wondered if she felt frustrated or angry. How could she not?

I also wondered if I would ever feel comfortable enough to ask her.

Whoa! Did she read my mind through the net? Shannon had just IM'd me.

It wasn't about this, though. It was about GoForIt.

To: Wordpainter
From: Wheelies
Re: Secret Identity
   Just so you quit whining about getting your story, I figured I'd let you know asap: Someone going by the name Aces logged off my website using the phrase "Till the next time." Could be GoForIt. The ISP is the same, too.

I didn't see why she had to get that zinger in about getting the story, but I chose to ignore it. After all, the point was that we might be onto our culprit.

To: Wheelies
From: Wordpainter
RE: Closing in.
   Excellent! I spotted an Aces in KidSpeak using that log-off, too. So Aces hangs where GoForIt did and uses the same sign-off. I have a feeling we got our GoForIt. Let's brainstorm with everyone else tomorrow to plan a sting operation.

I grinned. We were finally getting somewhere. I had no idea how we would actually prove that GoForIt was Aces and was behind the Alienheads fraud. I'd worry about that tomorrow. I wanted to hang on to this good mood.

Since I was on a roll of good luck, I figured I'd check into the *Real News* auction site. I hadn't checked all day. We must have made some money by now! Maybe there would even be a new bid on Gram's book.

Yay! Someone had added a dollar to the amount! The buyer was serious.

I was serious, too—about raising our numbers.

I brought the bid up another two dollars.

CHAPTER 12

Survey Says Good Moods Don't Last!

WHEN I WOKE up the next day, it was as if I had a mood reversal in my sleep. Everything yesterday was looking up. Today was another story.

It was Thursday. I had to hand in my story, or it wouldn't make it into next week's edition of *Real News*. We did layout on Friday, got the paper to the printer on Friday or Saturday, and Monday morning all the students at Trumbull had their newspaper.

And on Monday there would be a big blank front page where my Internet scam story was supposed to be. Okay. I had the story—kids being cheated via the school bb. But that was only half the story. I wanted to turn in a piece that took the reader from beginning to end— ending with Casey Smith's amazing revelation of the culprit's identity. It would be so much more satisfying if I could have that as my finale.

I had to solve the case now.

The word "how" went around and around in my head like a sock in a dryer. It banged around all through breakfast, giving me a headache.

Gram must have noticed. She gazed at me through the steam rising from her coffee cup. "Is everything all right?" she asked. "Have you gotten any more of that junk e-mail?"

The peanut butter on my toast clogged my mouth, so all I could do was mumble "Uh-uh."

"I take it that was a no," she said. "Good."

I swallowed and took a swig of milk. "Have you heard of cerebral palsy?" I asked. I figured I'd talk to Gram about one of the multitude of things weighing on me this morning.

"Now there's a non sequitur," Gram commented.

"I met this girl at school, and she has cerebral palsy," I explained.

"Shannon Butler?" Gram asked.

My eyes bugged. "How'd you know?"

"I've met her parents at PTA meetings. They seem very straightforward and reasonable. I spoke to her dad. They've had to do a lot of advocacy on Shannon's behalf."

"What do you mean?"

"If your child has special needs, there are a lot of obstacles and red tape to muddle through simply to get what the child is entitled to. In Shannon's case, they had insurance fights, problems with preschool, and even battles with some of her doctors, who simply didn't understand all the complexities because they weren't specialists. Shannon is lucky she has such strong parents. It can be overwhelming for parents to take care of so many things at once."

"Shannon has to cope with a lot of things, too," I mused. "But she doesn't act that way."

"That's good. She's strong too, I guess."

"She's Wheelies, from Wheelies's Web World," I added. "I had no idea that she had any kind of problem until she showed up at the *Real News* office."

"I take it that her true identity came as a surprise," Gram said.

I nodded. I didn't go into how freaked I had felt. I was hoping that would pass. Now that I had a better understanding of what was up with Shannon, maybe I could be a little more Casey-like around her.

"So is my book a best-seller?" Gram asked as she went to pour herself another cup of coffee.

I nearly choked on my milk. "Wh-why do you ask?" I sputtered.

She sat back down and poured on some syrup. "I'm just hoping you won't be disappointed by the results."

Another thing I didn't want to get into with Gram. My only hope was that the mysterious bidder would keep upping the price they were willing to pay until it made a decent showing.

"There have been some bids," I said completely truthfully. "There will be more before we close it down."

Gram looked amused. "I'm surprised there have been any bids at all. It's not exactly middle school material."

Before I left for school, I checked the auction site. Nothing had moved. No new bids, no final sales. Nothing. Next week was the final week of the auction. We didn't have much time.

I slung my backpack over my shoulder, kissed Gram good-bye and faced my world. It was full of deadlines. The auction. The newspaper. My social studies test next week that I hadn't started studying for. I would worry about that once I caught GoForIt, got my news story and beefed up the fund-raiser.

It looked as if I was going to have a busy morning. Basically, I needed to get this all done by the end of the day today.

Yeah. No problem.

◆◆◆

At school I headed straight to the *Real News* office. Because of everything going on I wanted to stay as linked as possible to the web. I wished I had one of those computers like Shannon's, with a wireless connection.

I took a quick look at KidSpeak to see if Aces was online. I still wanted to make sure Aces really was GoForIt, but I didn't exactly know how to do that. If I read more of the postings I might get a clue.

Bingo! Aces was back online, chatting with awesome123. They were both complaining about having too many chores to do.

Brainstorm. My brilliant thinking machine clicked in after being on vacation. Here was our ruse: lure Aces into bidding on chores posted on the *Real News* auction site. We'd immediately accept the bid and have a way to actually meet him. Or her, I reminded myself. After Wheelies surprised me by being Shannon, I knew better than to make any assumptions based on screen names.

I didn't exactly know how we'd link Aces to GoForIt and also to the Alienheads scam, but at least it would be a start.

The first thing I had to do was figure out what chore would grab Aces's attention most. I shifted in the chair and kept reading the chat. Aha! He was bummed that his mom insisted he clean out the garage before he could play football with friends on Sunday afternoon. The job was so huge he was sure he wouldn't get it done in time.

"There's the bait," I murmured.

I quickly posted an item to the *Real News* auction site. "Will clean your garage for best offer!" I wrote. Now I had to get Aces to go for it.

How could I do that without revealing that I knew that he was local? I drummed my fingers on the desk in front of the keyboard. After all, kids went into these chats from all over the country— all over the world, even. But GoForIt was using a local post office. I knew the creep lived somewhere in the general vicinity.

I didn't know if he had ever checked out the *Real News* auction site, so I would have to be really careful about setting this up.

I ran over the little we knew. Both GoForIt and Aces went to KidSpeak and to Wheelies's Web World. How could we use that information?

I e-mailed Shannon. I thought maybe she should add a link to *Real News* from her website. That might make it easier to lure Aces there.

She Instant Messaged me. Maybe you have some smarts after all, she wrote back. It's done.

Why the zing? She could have just said she had made the link. Was ragging me her new hobby?

The bell for homeroom rang, but I didn't move. I had to send Aces a message fast. I went into KidSpeak.

Wordpainter here. I'm a newbie, so spare me the flames.
I feel your pain, Aces. I'm overloaded with chores, too. Don't grown-ups realize we have lives? Anyway, I log into KidSpeak from this web page called Wheelies's Web World. It links to the Trumbull Middle School homepage. The school newspaper is running an online auction, and one of the things you can bid on is chores. So if you're in the Trumbull Middle School vicinity, check it out. You may make it to the game yet!

I sat back and waited for a response. None came. I glanced up at the clock. Yikes! The second bell must have already rang.

No wonder Aces didn't answer. If he went to Trumbull, he was already in homeroom.

I grabbed my stuff and ran up the stairs and down the hall. By the time I reached my homeroom, the bell for first period was ringing. I skidded to a stop.

I had missed all of homeroom, and if I didn't

run in there pronto, I would be marked as absent. But if I went in to try to fix the problem, I'd be late for first period. Keep heading to my homeroom or get to class? My head whipped back and forth as I looked up and down the hall. Which way should I go?

I made a decision. Better a tardy than an absence.

"I'm here! I'm here!" I exclaimed, running up to Ms. Wendall's desk

"You're awfully late, Casey," she said. "Do you have a note?"

A note. Hm. She had me stumped. "I was working on a story for *Real News* and I lost track of time. In fact, I got here extra early, so it's kind of unfair to mark me late. Only if I don't get going right now I'll be late for The Termina—I mean for math class. It won't happen again, I promise, just don't mark me absent, I'm here."

I actually said that all in one breath. I gasped for air when I was done. Ms. Wendall must have been impressed by my performance. Maybe she had hopes for me on the swim team or something since I had such amazing breath control. A hidden skill. Who knew?

"Okay, Casey. You can get to your next class. But you are on alert. You are accumulating late notices at quite a rate."

"Thank you." I darted out again and up another set of stairs. Man. I was putting in way too much exercise without getting any points for it. Why couldn't this count as gym class?

Throughout the day, I kept wanting to sneak over to *Real News* to see if Aces took the bait. But those bells were much too close together. And after the warning from my homeroom teacher I didn't want to risk adding more tardies to my record.

Finally it was lunchtime. I had brought leftovers from home, so I bypassed the cafeteria all together. I went straight to the office.

I was at the computer when Shannon came in. "Well, if it isn't the little news hound," she commented.

She said it in a condescending way, as if she was making fun of me. Why did she have such a problem with me? Then it hit me. Maybe Shannon was an Alienheads fan.

"So, did you manage to think about anyone other than yourself today?" She smirked at me.

I tried to stay polite. For all of two and a half seconds. "What's with you?" I snapped. "Where do you get off accusing me of all sorts of things? You don't know the first thing about me. We only met yesterday. So back off."

It was another one of those blurts. My face

flushed. I couldn't believe I lit into Shannon that way. I mean, she had enough problems as it was. She didn't need me picking on her. Even if she did start it.

Only she didn't seem even a little bit upset. Instead, she burst out laughing. Which made me mad again.

"You think that's funny?" I demanded. "How would you like it if someone decided they had you pegged in the first thirty seconds?"

"I don't like it at all," she said. "And it happens to me all the time." She grinned at me. "I was wondering how long it would take."

I was puzzled. "How long what would take?"

"For you to treat me like a human being."

"What are you talking about?" I protested. "I'm really nice to you."

"Exactly. Which is so not you."

I hated to admit it, but she had a point. Even *I* was making myself gag with how sweet and polite I had been to Shannon.

"Look," Shannon continued. "I've read your stuff and seen you in action. You're tough. Except with me. You've been walking on eggshells around me, treating me differently than you do other people. That's not what I want."

I flashed back to some of my research. One of the articles stressed how a kid may have cerebral palsy, but she's a kid first. Just like any other kid. That wasn't how I was treating Shannon. I was treating her like just a condition, not a person.

"You're right," I admitted. "And I'm not just saying that because you're in a wheelchair."

"Thanks," she said.

"You get that a lot, don't you?" I asked. "People acting all weird around you."

"Yeah," she said. "It gets old real fast. That's why the first thing I do is lay it out. This is who I am. The four-one-one on the wheelchair, the special computer. After that, though, it's up to them."

I nodded. "There's only so far you can bend over backwards for other people."

"Especially me. Since I can't bend over backwards at all."

For a second I stared at her.

"Joke, Casey. Lighten up."

"Sorry. It's just . . . I don't know if I could have your attitude. You seem so . . . adjusted. More than some kids I know without cerebral palsy."

"Don't get me wrong. I have bad days, too," Shannon said. "I don't want to be the poster child for sainthood or anything."

"No one would confuse Wheelies with a saint," I told her. "You get up to some wicked slamming on that website."

She shot me a pleased grin. "I'm glad you like it. You know, I think you're a really good writer. So it means a lot to me that you think the web page is good."

"Good?" I repeated. "It totally rocks. I've always thought you should write for *Real News,* except I think you'd scare Megan."

"She is pretty prissy, isn't she. She's like the Sugar Plum Fairy."

I laughed. "Were we separated at birth? I feel like I need dark glasses to take all that pink."

Shannon nodded. "She makes me think of bubble gum."

"You are so on my wavelength," I said. "But I guessed that from the site."

"That's one of the reasons I'm so into the web," Shannon admitted. "It allows people to get to know me without this getting in the way." She banged her hand against the side of the wheelchair. "Like it did with you."

I bit my lip. I wasn't sure how to apologize for my strangeness at the beginning with Shannon.

"You should write about that for *Real News,*" a voice said behind us.

Megan. Gulp. How much had she heard?

"Write about what?" Shannon said. I could tell she was also worried about what Megan might have heard.

Megan came in and sat at Dalmation Station. "I didn't mean to eavesdrop. But I think the point you just made, about the web being a way to get to know one another without prejudices, would be a good one. Especially since we're going to be writing about the dangers of the anonymity. You're the flip side of that argument."

"She's right," I told Shannon. "It would be a great angle."

"I'll think about it," Shannon said. "But I'm pretty busy with Wheelies's Web World."

It occurred to me that if she wrote about the benefit of being anonymous, she wouldn't be anonymous anymore. I didn't think she would want to give that up.

"So how is the fraud story coming?" Megan asked.

Saved by the bell. I didn't want to admit that so far all I had were hunches and hopes. "I'll bring you up to speed at the meeting after classes today," I promised. "I can't be late—I've already received far too many marks against me today."

"Okay."

"I need to go, too," Shannon said. She wheeled herself out of the room as I gathered up my books.

I dashed to English class. If Aces had responded to the bait, Shannon would have told me. So far, zilch.

What if he didn't go for it? What if Aces guessed we were onto him? Or lived too far away to think it would be likely we'd do the chores? What if Aces wasn't GoForIt?

What if what it what if . . .

Aaaggghhhh!!!

Finally, *finally*, classes were over. I hurried to the *Real News* office and checked the site.

"We got him!" I cried.

"Got who?" Ringo asked.

I whirled around. I had been so focused on getting at the computer, I hadn't noticed him sitting on the floor in the corner. "Aces bid on the garage-cleaning offer I posted."

"So the auction is going better," he asked. "Decent. How's my cookbook doing?"

"No, you don't get it." I filled Ringo in on how Shannon and I laid a trap for Aces. While I was explaining the sting operation, the rest of the staff came in. So did Tyler and Shannon.

"Okay, here's the deal," I declared. I felt like the top cop laying it out for my detectives. "We need to verify that Aces is actually GoForIt. And we have to prove that GoForIt was selling fake Alienheads. I'm not exactly sure how we're going to do that, but getting into his house is a great first step."

"Casey, we need to know what's running

on the front page," Megan reminded me. "We don't know if this is going to give us the story or not."

She was right. "Okay. Let me tell Aces we have to do it today. Then I'll write up the story this afternoon. If I have to, I'll e-mail it in tonight so it will be here for edit and layout first thing tomorrow morning."

"Good idea," Shannon said. "Answer the e-mail."

I posted a message, explaining that we were so booked with garage-cleaning appointments that the only time available would be today. Because of that, I told him, we were willing to forgo the usual rules. Instead of having to give us the money up front, he could pay us after the job. I didn't want anything to slow us down.

Excellent. Aces bit. He e-mailed me his real name: Jack Henson. And his real address: just four blocks from the post office on Main Street.

"Ready, troops?" I asked. Everyone nodded.

Everyone except Megan. "Casey," she protested. "What if you're wrong? What if this Jack isn't the one selling fake Alienheads? What will we put on the front page?"

"Please, please, please, just hold the page," I begged. I didn't have an answer to her objections, so I figured the sheer pleasure of watching me beg would get her to give in. "Please?" I wheedled again.

She sighed. "Okay." Then she did something that surprised me. She snapped her notebook shut and stood up. "Let's go get this creep!" she declared. She glanced down at her clothes. "I just hope the garage isn't too messy," she commented. "I'm not exactly dressed for chores."

Bait Gives Off Fishy Odor!

I FINALLY HAD sympathy for Megan. Selling chores was a good idea, until you had to do them. We had twenty bids on the bait we set for Aces. That was great for *Real News*. But it would mean twenty garages to clean out. I figured I'd broach that subject later. The first priority was to get this front-page story.

Luckily, the entire *Real News* staff agreed to come along. Tyler and Gary would come in handy. Shannon stayed behind. She decided to write that piece on the positive aspects of the Internet for us. She was going to work on it while we were cleaning up.

We hurried to Jack's house. I started to feel nervous. I was certain that Aces was a kid—the complaint about his parents made that obvious—

but still he was a kid willing to commit a serious crime. Internet fraud was just as serious as any other kind of fraud. Which was probably why Principal Nachman clamped down on the student bb so fast. If the rip-off was big enough, the culprit could even go to jail. There are whole crime units devoted to scoping out this stuff.

I was secretly glad I wasn't tackling this story alone. Don't get me wrong—I was thrilled that the story was this big, this serious, this *real*. I was simply glad to have company along. Going into the house of a stranger was bad enough. Going into a house of a suspected scam-artist—that was probably at the top of the list of things kids should never do.

Which was why I was kind of startled that Megan had joined us. She's usually the Princess of Rules. She even waited until the light turned green before crossing the street. I mean, she wouldn't even step off the curb.

We huddled at the mailbox: Toni, Gary, Megan, Ringo, Tyler and me. We must have made some sight. Like a rogue field trip gone awry or something. Megan all preppiness, Ringo in tie-dye, Toni in wide-legged khakis and combat boots, Gary dressed in his usual jock attire. Then there were understated Tyler and me. In fact, we had on matching turtlenecks, as if we had planned it or something.

I consulted the piece of paper I had scrawled Jack's address on. I squinted at the house. And the mailbox. I wanted to be super-duper sure.

"Come on, Casey, it's cold out here," Toni complained. "Get with it."

Somewhere along the way Toni had decided to speak to me again. It was one of those things I decided not to question, just accept.

"This is it," I whispered.

"Casey, if you go all *Mission Impossible* the dude's going to suspect something," Gary scolded.

I shoved the paper into my jeans pocket. "This is it. Let's go. Now everybody act normal," I instructed.

"Take your own advice," Toni muttered.

I put my hands on my hips. "You know, people, if it wasn't for me, we wouldn't be here."

"Out here in the cold," Toni complained.

"We don't know if this is even where we need to be," Megan reminded me. "We don't know if Jack *is* GoForIt."

Thanks a lot, I thought. Make my anxiety level hit the roof.

"We're moving in," Gary declared.

We walked up to the front door. It just looked like an ordinary door. Did an Internet scammer live back there?

I rang the doorbell.

A tall boy answered the door. "Yeah?" he asked.

"Are you Jack Hensen?" I asked.

He looked familiar. I was pretty sure he was an eighth grader at Trumbull. I could kind of picture him at one of the lunchroom tables reserved for the super-cool.

"Yeah. Why?"

If being suspicious and unfriendly was a sign of guilt, then we had our guy. I wondered if he recognized Toni. She was a pretty visible kid. Then I remembered that he probably only knew her by her screen name, HotStuff.

Tyler nudged me.

"We're from *Real News,*" I said. "We're here to clean your garage." And finger you as an Internet scam artist, I added telepathically.

"I didn't realize you were squirts," Jack said. He wore baggy jeans that drooped low on his hips, and an oversized T-shirt. It made his arms look really long and scrawny. "Hope you're up to the job."

"It'll be worth it," I said. "I promised."

Especially for us, I thought. Cleaning your garage will be worth that front-page story.

The guy's jaw stuck out as he gave us the once over. "Well, you're better than nothing. That garage stands between me and my game on Sunday."

"We should get started," I said. This guy was standing between me and my story.

Jack led us around to the garage.

"I can see why your mom is on your case," Tyler commented.

The garage was a complete and total mess. There was barely room for a car in there. Stacks of papers, bags of recycling, old toys, old sports equipment, old everything.

"Have you considered donating to the *Real News* auction?" Megan asked.

I was in awe. We were here to catch a bad guy, and Megan was on the ball enough to also try to get a donation out of it. Maybe she did care about what happened with the fund-raiser.

I tried not to smirk. It would be like a bonus— two for the price of one. Actually three. One, he'd pay us for cleaning the garage. Two, we'd sell his useable junk for the auction. Three, I'd get my story.

The only problems of course were: A. We had to actually prove he was GoForIt, and B. We had to actually clean the garage.

I had forgotten about that part.

"We could use some trash bags, paper towels, maybe some cleaning stuff?" Megan said to Jack.

"You've done this before," Gary observed.

"It seems to be a really popular chore for the yearbook committee to do," she explained. "I've got it down."

Jack went into the house through the door at the back of the garage. He came back out with supplies.

"We'll make piles in the driveway," Megan explained to Jack. "That way we won't accidentally throw out anything you still want. And you can approve what we take away as donations."

"You can have any of the toys," Jack said. "Ask me about the equipment. My mom said to get rid of any of the broken stuff, since most of it's been out here forever and isn't ever going to get fixed."

"Will do," Gary said.

"Just get it done, okay?" Jack said. "You need to be out of here before my mom gets back at six." He slammed back into the house.

I figured he was going to pass off our work as his own. We'd do all the work, he'd take all the credit. Jack was sounding more and more like our dude. He was fitting the profile. Arrogant. Didn't mind cheating, since he was obviously going to lie about who cleaned the garage.

"Now what do we do?" Megan turned to me. "This is your story. Any suggestions on how to get it?"

I scanned the garage. It was piled high with junk. "First thing, we don't get killed. Some of those piles look pretty precarious."

Toni perched on a pile of recycling bags. "We have to actually clean this place?"

"Of course," Megan replied. "We said we would. And we still don't know if Jack is our culprit. We can't blow it off just because we *think* he might be guilty. That would make *Real News* look bad."

She stepped around some oozing paint cans. "I'm really not dressed for this." She gazed down at her pale pink skirt and ballet slippers. She spotted a pile of clothing sitting on a shelf. She daintily picked through the stuff, holding it away from her body with the tips of her fingers. "I'm sure Jack wouldn't mind if I borrowed this." She slipped into a man's button-down shirt. It hung down below her skirt, completely covering her color-coordinated outfit.

"Now that we've solved Megan's fashion crisis, can we get started?" I said.

"Remember to set aside anything that might be sellable," Megan added.

We got to work. We pulled everything off the shelves and put it on the floor. We filled three trash bags with paint cans and broken appliances.

We didn't find anything that connected Jack to the scam.

Maybe the evidence is inside, I thought.

I wiped my grimy hands on my jeans. We all looked really messy. Ringo had paint in his hair. He must have gotten it on his hands and then scratched his head or something.

I went into the house. I figured if Jack caught me, I'd tell him I was looking for the bathroom. That would sound legit. And I looked messy enough to convince him we were really there to clean out his garage.

What would be a clue? I wondered. I snuck down the hallway. I peeked into a closet. All I found were towels.

How could I prove that Jack ripped off those kids? I stood in the living room with my hands on my hips. I bit my lip, thinking hard. I shook my head. What was I looking for? Boxes of fake Alienheads? Stashes of cash?

The best shot I had at finding incriminating evidence would be in Jack's room. Yeah. Like he was going to let me rifle though his stuff.

I had to do the best I could. I was after this story. I just had to let it take me wherever it took me.

I tiptoed down the hallway. I wanted to catch Jack by surprise. I didn't want to give him the chance to hide anything.

I flung open the door.

Oops. It was definitely a grown-up's bedroom. Super neat. Big bed. Bills on the dresser and magazines on health on a chair. I checked it out anyway. I peeked into the closet. The bathroom. Nothing linking Jack to the scam.

I went back to the hallway and headed for the door at the other end. My sneakers didn't make any noise on the polished wood floor.

This time, I cracked the door open a tiny bit. Jack sat at his desk with his back to me. I nearly gasped.

Jack's room made mine look like something out of a Martha Stewart magazine.

The place was a serious pigsty. I was glad we were only cleaning the garage. It was a much easier job to tackle.

I scanned as much of the room as I could see through the crack in the door. But the range was too narrow. I pushed the door open a few more inches.

More mess. Mess as far as the eye could see.

I did notice a major computer hookup. This guy was wired. He was also wearing a headset. No wonder he didn't hear the door creak open.

I felt bold. I pushed the door open even more and took a step into the room.

Oops! A pile of books toppled over.

Jack swiveled around in his chair. "What are

you doing in my room?" he demanded.

I went to my cover story. "I was looking for the bathroom."

"This isn't it."

"I figured that out. So which door is it?" I asked.

Jack got up from his chair and shoved me out the door. "Down there. You passed it on the way in from the garage. Are you almost finished out there?"

"Almost," I fibbed.

I went into the bathroom to keep him from getting suspicious that I had been snooping. I flushed the toilet and then went back out to the garage.

"What do you think you're doing?" Gary snapped. "This was your idea, and you leave us here to do all the work?"

"I was working!" I retorted. "The hard work of solving this crime."

Toni leaned against a shaky bookshelf. "Give it up," she said. "We're getting nowhere."

"Don't say that!" I said. I had to get this story. Not only did I need a front-page story, I also needed to keep my pride.

How we were going to get the evidence we needed?

"Would you at least pretend to help?" Gary said.

I wished he would stop carping on me in front of Tyler. I didn't want Tyler to think I was a slacker.

"I am helping, okay?" I picked up three full recycling bags. "See?" I trudged out of the garage to bring the bags to the cans. "How am I going to get GoForIt?" I muttered. I was so frustrated I couldn't stop muttering to myself. I slammed the bags down onto the sidewalk.

Just great. The bottom bag broke. I guess I didn't even know my own strength. Or irritation level.

Now I'd have to repack all those papers.

I went back into the garage and grabbed the box of recycling bags. I went back to the burst bag and knelt down. I grabbed a fistful of envelopes and papers and shoved them into the new bag.

I had shoveled in a batch of the papers when one of the big envelopes got caught on the edge of the bag. As I fiddled with it, I glanced down at the address.

"Bingo!" I shouted. I jumped up and down, waving the envelope.

No one in the garage paid any attention to me. I dashed back into the garage. "Look!" I cried. "I did it! I found the evidence."

They dropped everything and gathered around me. "What do you mean?" Megan asked.

I held out the envelope. "Check out the address."

"P.O. box number four-seventeen," Tyler read. "Same zip code." He grinned at me. "You did it, all right."

"That's the address we sent our money to," Toni murmured

"These are addressed to someone named Victoria Hensen," Gary pointed out.

"That's probably Jack's mom," I said. "I bet Jack was using his mom's P.O. box without her knowing it. And I think we should go find out exactly how he pulled off this little scam."

"And get our money back," Toni added.

Megan had dashed out to the broken bag. She darted back into the garage. "I found a batch more. I was hoping to find one with Toni or Tyler's return address, but I didn't."

"These are good enough to confront Jack with," I assured her. "Let's go."

We marched into the house and into Jack's room. I didn't bother to knock.

He whirled around in his chair. "Are you done already?" he asked.

"We're not," I informed him. "But you are."

"What are you talking about?" Jack said. He didn't look even the slightest bit worried. I was about to change that.

"Gotcha, GoForIt," I said.

His eyes registered the tiniest bit of surprise. He covered quickly. "Huh?"

I waved the envelopes in front of him. "You've been cheating kids by selling fake Alienheads. Here's the proof."

Jack raised an eyebrow. "You are so freaked."

"These envelopes were sent to the same post office box used to do the scam," I said.

"You don't know what you're talking about." He turned back around to his computer. "Just finish the garage and get out."

My mouth dropped open. He played it so cool. We had him dead to rights and he still denied it. I pressed harder. "Did you know that using the mail to commit fraud is a federal offense?"

Jack didn't turn around. I did notice that the back of his neck got kind of red and his left foot started to jiggle.

Good. I wanted to see this guy squirm.

"Well, lookie here," Tyler said. I turned and saw that Tyler had been rummaging around in a box in the corner. He pulled out a big Alienheads figurine. He squeezed its feet. Nothing happened.

"Let me see," Toni said. Tyler tossed her the Alienhead. She flipped it upside down. "It's fake," she declared. "The logo is wrong."

Jack slumped in his chair. "Okay, okay," he

mumbled. "You're right. You got me." He turned around to face us. "What are you going to do about it?"

"Tell me something," I asked. "How did you pull it off?"

"My mom has a home business. One of my jobs is to pick up the mail. So I knew I'd always see the mail before she did."

"Why did you do it?" Toni demanded. "Why would you rip off other kids?"

"For the money," Gary answered for Jack. "Right, dude?"

"Not exactly," Jack replied. He slammed a fist on the back of his chair. "Man, this totally rots."

"No, buddy, *you* totally rot," Toni snapped.

"You don't get it. I got ripped off. That's where I got all the stupid Alienheads to begin with. There were really expensive, too."

"Like a few hundred bucks' worth, I'd guess," Gary said. "You were selling the priciest ones."

Jack nodded. "I used my mom's credit card. Man, did I ever get busted on that. To pay her back, I came up with the idea of selling the stupid things."

"Why didn't you report it?" I asked.

He looked sheepish. "I didn't tell my mom that they were fake. She was so mad, and giving me all these lectures, I really didn't want to give her any more ammunition."

"So because something bad happened to you, you just turned around and did it to some other kids?" I said. "That totally blows chunks."

Jack sighed. "I know. But I thought maybe the kids wouldn't notice they weren't real."

Toni snorted. "As if. If you're into Alienheads, you're all the way into them."

"Well, you are now double-busted," I informed him. "You had better go confess all. This little scam of yours is going to be the front page of *Real News* on Monday."

CHAPTER 14

High Fives Endanger Students' Health!

WE TUMBLED BACK out to the garage, totally giddy. We contained ourselves as best we could. Jack was in so much trouble we didn't think it would be too cool to jump for joy in front of him.

"We did it!" I cried. "I have my front-page story!"

"Way to go, Casey!" Tyler shouted. He and I tried to slap high fives. The only problem was I jumped up to reach his hand and he bent down. So I smacked him on the side of the head and he hit me on the chin.

"Ow!" I said with a grin.

"Back at you," Tyler said, smiling.

Jack had broken open his cash box and paid back every penny of the money he had taken

156

from Tyler, Toni, and Ben. We warned him that he had better pay back any other kids he had ripped off—it might make him be in a little less trouble.

"Let's get this story in," I declared. I headed toward the street. No one followed. I turned around. "What?"

"We can't just leave this mess," Megan said. "Look at this place."

It looked even worse than when we started. Piles of junk lay out in the driveway, and there wasn't any room for a car to drive in.

"But I have to get the story written," I protested. "The layout. The deadlines."

Megan blew a grimy strand of blond hair out of her face. She took a deep breath. "Okay. You go back to school and write up the story. We'll finish up here."

"Why does she get to blow off the work?" Gary complained.

"Because I'm the one with the scoop," I said.

"Go, before we change our minds," Tyler warned.

"Okay, okay, I'll see you back at school. Shannon might still be there. Maybe she can help with the edit and layout."

"Good job," Megan called after me.

I beamed all the way back to school. Just as I had hoped, Shannon was still in the *Real News* office.

"Judging from your expression, I'd say you got your story," she said.

"And everyone's money back, too." I wanted her to know I was capable of thinking about other people.

I sat down at the computer. Shannon wheeled up beside me. "I got most of my story done," she said.

"Great."

"Where are the others?"

"Cleaning the garage."

This was one of those stories that wrote itself. It worked really well with the Internet issues story that I wrote, too.

By the time we had finished, Shannon and I had to leave or we'd have ended up having a sleepover at Trumbull. There was still the lay-out to do, and I knew Megan would kill me if I declared the story ready without letting her read it first. From home I sent an e-mail around asking everyone to meet first thing in the morning, before classes. I sent one to Shannon, too, since she had been so important in helping me crack the story.

◆ ◆ ◆

The next morning everyone was already there when I got in—everyone but Shannon. They all applauded when I walked in. Totally cool. I took a little bow.

"We read the story," Megan said. "It's really good."

"So what happened after I left?" I asked, sliding into a chair at Dalmatian Station. "Did Jack's mom come home?"

"I almost feel sorry for the slacker," Toni commented. "Almost."

"He was so busted on so many levels," Gary said. "First, his mom was bugged that he pawned the garage off on us."

"I told her it was for a good cause," Megan said. "Trying to soften the blow a little."

"And to make sure we got paid for our trouble," Gary added.

Megan grinned. "That, too."

"When she asked him how he planned to pay us, well, everything fell apart. The whole sad story came out." Toni shook her head. "Nothing more pathetic than a snotty kid crying in front of kids he cheated."

"How much trouble is he in?" I asked.

"It's a federal offense," Ringo explained,

159

"whether the kids who got ripped off press charges or not."

"He's paying everyone back," Megan reported. "And they're reporting the original rip-off to the authorities."

"We have to add that to the story," I said. I opened the file and made final adjustments to the story. It was a scorcher.

While I was at the computer, I checked on the auction site. "Awesome!" I exclaimed. The numbers were way up.

I turned around in the chair. "Ringo, your cookbook is a hit!"

"I know. I'm thinking of doing a sequel."

"I see you finally made a contribution," I said to Megan.

"Well, the chores worked so well for the yearbook, why not go for it for *Real News?*"

"How are you going to juggle everything?" Gary asked.

"The yearbook chores are pretty much done," Megan said. "Besides, I'm super-organized."

"That's an understatement," I commented. I turned back to check on the most important item: Gram's book.

My mouth dropped open. It had gone up to twenty dollars! I quickly added another two dollars to the bid. I had to see how much higher it would go.

"And you all doubted me." I got up and strolled around the table. "You see? My grandmother's book is a total success! Twenty-two dollars today, tomorrow, who knows? How high will it go?"

I plopped down at the head of the table, tipped back my chair and put my feet up. "There are some students at Trumbull with taste. Smarts. Brains. Just because you didn't recognize the brilliance of my contribution—"

Toni cut me off. "Okay, girl. You can quit gloating. I know why the bid went so high."

"Sure," I told her. "Because who wouldn't want an autographed copy of an important book by a prize-winning journalist?"

"No," Toni countered. "It was because I felt bad about slamming you all the time when you were working really hard to solve the case. So I made that twenty-dollar bid."

I gaped at her.

So did Gary. "I was the one who bid fifteen dollars," he confessed.

"What?" I squeaked. "Who else made pity bids on Gram's book?" I glanced around the table.

Ringo and Megan raised their hands.

"We knew how much it mattered to you," Megan explained. "I was afraid you would be really disappointed if you didn't get any bids."

"It worked. Someone added to Toni's bid," Ringo pointed out.

I smacked my forehead. "Oh man! Those extra two dollars were mine. I owe *Real News* twenty-two dollars. I was the last one to bid."

Toni jingled her bracelets. "I tell you what, girl. I'll buy the book. I feel flush. I got my money back from Jack, thanks to you. If it wasn't for you staying on the case, I'd have kissed the money bye-bye for good. It's going to a good cause, right?"

I beamed at her. "Right."

Shannon wheeled herself into the room.

"You did a great job on that story," Megan complimented her. "Have you thought more about writing for us?"

"I've thought about it," Shannon replied. "I'm not up for that, but let me suggest something else. Why don't I maintain a web page for *Real News?* You could use it to conduct surveys. It could be another way to write to the 'JAM' column. And you can let kids know what's coming up."

"That's an excellent idea," I said.

"You know, you really should do an online

newspaper instead," Shannon continued. "Print is so last millennium."

I laughed out loud. I caught Megan's eye.

"Get real!" we chimed together.

My Word
by Linda Ellerbee

MY NAME IS LINDA ELLERBEE. As you know, some of the characters in the Get Real series are sort of based on real people. For instance, Casey is sort of based on me, but there's a little of Gram in me, too. Megan is based on a couple of kids I've known and Ringo is kind of like another kid I know. But in this particular book, there's a new character, Shannon, who lives her life in a wheelchair. This character is definitely based on a real person, whose name also happens to be Shannon.

I met Shannon several years ago when *Nick News* produced a television special called "What Are You Staring At?" It was a show about people with physical disabilities. Shannon (the real one) was one of the kids on the special. She has cerebral palsy. Her directness, her intelligence and her industrial-strength sense of humor blew us away. That, and her courage. You see, Shannon isn't going to go through life on anyone's terms but her own. She fights for her rights and isn't afraid of making a scene when a scene is what is called for. She's my kind of girl.

In 1999, we invited Shannon back for another *Nick News* show. Several years had passed. Shannon was now thirteen. I said to her, "Shannon, last time you were here you told us you meant to change the world. Have you?"

"Well," Shannon said, "I don't know if I've changed the world, but if I've changed how some people see me, that will do."

My friend Shannon continues to challenge the rest of us every day of her life. She makes us look past the chair, past the disease, and see the person. She mocks us about our own prejudices, and our own ignorance. She forces us to see what she can do, not what she can't do. She changes us by changing how we see her. And so I wanted to include a character like her in this series.

The real life Shannon is one of my heroes. I suspect she's going to be one of Casey's heroes, too. Maybe even one of yours.

It's not easy being "different," but with kids like Shannon to lead us, can we truly learn to celebrate these differences? Can you make that happen?

Get real.